Her eyelids snapped open, expression foggy with sleep.

"Good morning," he said, his voice gravelly and deep.

She blinked. Her hand gripped his chest hair. She moved her leg slightly against his hip. Her eyes widened; her cheeks reddened.

The pulse at the base of her throat accelerated. Her pupils dilated.

She didn't move. She pressed closer.

His heart leaped away. The burn simmering inside his gut exploded. He shook with the effort to maintain control.

He couldn't look away. She'd captured him with her gaze. He held his breath.

"Rafe," she whispered. Her tongue dampened her lips.

"You should move." He cleared his throat. "Or I should."

She lifted her hand from the bare skin of his chest. She nodded in agreement, tossing a wave of disappointment and resignation through him.

He allowed his hands to fall back to the sheets. All for the best. But right now he had to get away from here. He needed that shower or to dunk himself into a tub of ice. "I think I'd better—"

"Don't think," Sierra whispered.

SAN ANTONIO SECRET

ROBIN PERINI

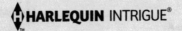

For my agent, Jill Marsal, and my editor, Allison Lyons.

I'm blessed to have you in my corner during the good times
and the bad.

Thank you. For everything.

ISBN-13: 978-0-373-75654-4

San Antonio Secret

Copyright © 2016 by Robin L. Perini

Recycling programs
for this product may
not exist in your area.

Printed in U.S.A.

www.Harlequin.com

Award-winning author **Robin Perini**'s love of heart-stopping suspense and poignant romance, coupled with her adoration of high-tech weaponry and covert ops, encouraged her secret inner commando to take on the challenge of writing romantic suspense novels. Robin loves to interact with readers. You can catch her on her website, www.robinperini.com, and on several major social-networking sites, or write to her at PO Box 50472, Albuquerque, NM 87181-0472.

Books by Robin Perini

Harlequin Intrigue

Finding Her Son
Cowboy in the Crossfire
Christmas Conspiracy
Undercover Texas
The Cradle Consipiracy
Secret Obsession
Christmas Justice
San Antonio Secret

CAST OF CHARACTERS

Sierra Bradford—After her best friend and goddaughter are kidnapped, Sierra will do anything to save them, even go undercover at the rodeo with the man who broke her heart.

Rafe Vargas—Known as the covert operative who succeeds at the assignments that no one else will risk, Rafe never expected his toughest job would be to work side by side on an investigation with the woman he can never have.

Mallory and Chloe Harrigan—When Mallory discovered missing money at the rodeo, she had no idea she'd put a target on herself and her five-year-old daughter.

Bud Harrigan—Vowing to force his wife and daughter to return to him, has this ex-husband done the unthinkable and kidnapped them to reconstruct his family?

Zane Westin—With computer skills second to none, Zane always finds his mark, but can he find a woman and child before it's too late?

Harlen Anderson—This rodeo veterinarian may hold the key to the missing woman and child—if his own secrets don't get in the way.

John Beckel—He owns the rodeo, but did he embezzle from his own company, frame Mallory and orchestrate her kidnapping, or is he also a victim?

Warren Beckel—The rodeo's silent partner, he defends his brother no matter what the evidence reveals.

Detective Cade Foster—The only person in the San Antonio Police Department who Rafe and Sierra trust, has he now betrayed his badge in the worst way?

Covert Technology Confidential (CTC)—This organization of elite operatives helps those who have run out of options. Can they uncover the corruption at the rodeo before a woman and child run out of time?

Prologue

Dreary November clouds hung low and menacing, blocking out the clear blue of the Denver sky. Small pricks of ice laced the air, but Rafe Vargas didn't feel the cold, even as a puff of visible breath escaped his lips. His focus lasered on the door of the warehouse.

Most of the block was deserted, but orange caution tape and cones peppered the streets. Not surprising. Rafe didn't have to walk inside the building to know dynamite and detonator cords crisscrossed the location. This entire block of downtown had been scheduled to be dust in a matter of minutes. Covert Technology Confidential's resident geek, Zane Westin, better be right about the target's coordinates.

Rafe tugged the stocking cap around his ears to camouflage his identity, bowing his head to avoid providing the surveillance camera a clear image of the patch covering his left eye. That psycho serial killer Archimedes needed to believe the man currently sneaking into the building was Rafe's best friend and fellow CTC operative, Noah Bradford, otherwise two women might die: the woman Noah guarded and had fallen in love with, and the one Rafe had flown across the country to rescue, Noah's sister, Sierra.

Archimedes was attempting to use her as leverage to stop Noah's investigation. Rafe wasn't about to let that happen, but if he had a prayer of getting her out alive, he had to locate her first.

Then again, if he found Sierra in time to save her life, he might have to kill her. Or kiss her until neither one of them could breathe—the way he'd wanted to from the day they'd met.

Either choice made his gut ache. Best friends' sisters were off-limits for one. Secondly, and more immediately, Archimedes liked to play deadly games, and he didn't give a rip about collateral damage. He might just murder Sierra for the satisfaction of proving he could.

Rafe palmed his Kimber 1911 and slipped through the warehouse door. He eyed a camera and ducked behind a large concrete support in a visual dead zone. That ominous and all-too-familiar tingle skittered down Rafe's spine. He had no doubt Archimedes was watching. The man was a sick voyeur, and the moment Rafe showed himself, the serial killer would know.

"We're clear," a worker in a yellow hard hat called across the room to the blaster.

"Then let's get out of here. This sucker's going to collapse like a pancake."

The men hurried out, slamming a metal door behind them. The clang echoed through the empty building.

Rafe checked his GPS and surveyed the open area. Yep. Drilled holes stuffed with dynamite dotted columns throughout the place. No one knew the order was on hold.

They had to keep it that way. Until he found Sierra.

He followed the trail from one of the dynamite cluster's detonation cables until a *second* set of wiring caught his attention.

Well, damn and double damn.

Archimedes had been here.

Military grade dets, not used for civilian demolition. No wonder the serial killer had oozed that smug, I-know-more-than-I'm-telling arrogance during their last communication. He'd rigged the existing wire to give him complete control. Even if the demolition expert didn't set off the charge, Archimedes could. And would.

Sierra.

Rafe's heart thudded hard against his chest. He glanced at his watch. Hell, no. Five minutes.

If he shot out the cameras, Archimedes might detonate early. Rafe tapped his earpiece. "Zane, you're sure about those coordinates?"

"Unless Archimedes spoofed them. And he could have. I'd give it fifty-fifty."

"Not good enough." CTC's surveillance expert was the best Rafe had ever worked with. There had to be a way. "If the place doesn't blow, Archimedes is going to set off the dynamite. Can you jam the detonation signal?"

"I don't have the time to crack his encryption." A curse erupted from Zane. "He's one step ahead of us. Again."

"What about the cameras?"

"If I disrupt them, he'll know." A drumming sounded through the phone. "Maybe…okay, it'll just be a minute, but I have an idea."

"You don't have a minute," Rafe snapped.

A blur of tapping sounded through the phone. "If I loop the camera feed—"

"He won't know I'm here. Very Hollywood thriller of you."

"I try. It's not going to be pretty, though. If he's watching closely enough, he'll be able to tell."

"Do it."

"I already started," Zane said. "A half minute more."

The seconds ticked by. Rafe studied the path to Sierra's coordinates, timing it in his head.

"That's as good as it'll get," Zane said. "Go."

Rafe catapulted from his hiding place and raced across the large concrete building. He skidded to a halt in front of a closed metal door and turned the knob. Locked. "Sierra. I'm coming for you," he shouted.

He backed up and slammed his foot against the barrier with all his weight behind him. The door bent, but didn't open. Another kick. A third. A fourth. It wouldn't give way.

A loud ticking echoed in his head, his internal clock counting down the seconds. This wasn't working, and Archimedes could discover the deception at any moment.

A large spread of debris littered the floor nearby. A piece of rusted rebar stuck out from one heap. Rafe clutched it in his hand and wedged the end in a small crack created by his assault. With a loud groan he pried the door open.

"Sierra?"

He peered through the opening.

Empty. A mound of wiring and debris filled the small room.

What the hell?

"She's not here, Zane. Am I even in the right warehouse?"

"According to my data, she has to be within a few feet," he said.

Ninety seconds.

Normally Rafe's body grew ultracalm the more perilous the operation, but this was Sierra. His palms grew damp, a bead of sweat trailed down his temple. Where the hell was she?

He rounded a corner and on the opposite wall facing the room he'd just entered, he found another door. The metal was bent, slightly off center.

He jammed in the rebar and pried it open. Sierra lay in the small, cramped closet, feet bound, mouth duct-taped, her shirt splayed open, and blood trickling from a carving of the infinity symbol on her upper left breast.

Her eyes widened.

"Got her," he said into his comm. He knelt beside her, tugging her shirt closed and slicing through her bindings with his Bowie. "You're one tough woman to find."

Her body trembled, and she shrank from his touch.

"Easy does it." As carefully as he could, he pulled off the tape. "Can you walk?"

"I can try," her husky voice croaked. She swiped at her eyes and fought to sit up.

"We can't wait to find out." He scooped her into his arms and pushed out of her tiny prison. He bolted toward the door. She clung to his neck. A few feet from the exit a loud explosion shuddered the building. Smoke billowed at him, rolling in the waves of a nightmare.

Visibility went nil.

Rafe felt for the handle of the door and clutched the metal. He yanked it open. The ground shook beneath him. Legs pumping hard, he carried Sierra as far as he could.

They wouldn't make it.

The building pancaked behind them, a sonic boom knocking him off his feet. The force slammed them to the ground.

He landed on top of her, and she grunted at the force of his weight. Before he could check on her injuries, a deluge of debris shot out with the force of an artillery bombardment. Rafe shielded her with his body, hoping his Kevlar was enough protection. Dirt, dust, metal and glass battered them both, pummeling them as if they'd been tossed into the heart of a tornado.

The world had turned to hell, and he had no idea if they'd survive or end up buried alive.

Archimedes might very well get exactly what he wanted.

THE MOTEL ROOM was a dump. Clean, but still a dump. Rafe lay on the rickety, regular-size bed and stared at the water-stained ceiling, his Kimber within reach on the bedside table. A glint of early-morning light peeked between the cheap blinds, providing just enough visibility for Rafe to study, yet again, the odd patterns the discolorations had created. He needed the distraction.

His body thrummed with tension, with unrelenting longing. Sometime during her sleep, Sierra Bradford had worked her way across the too-small bed and settled on top of him, her soft, toasty body pinning his legs and chest to the mattress.

Nestled against him, she was killing him with every curve, every inch of flesh. Her warm, even breath burned a hole in his chest. Her brown hair, luxurious to the touch, cascaded over his shoulder. The clean soap and hint of lilac lotion she favored danced a seduction on his senses.

Just one small movement of his hand and he could caress her silky skin. He didn't know how much longer he could take the torture.

He fisted the rough sheets and closed his eyes against the temptation. He wanted to groan aloud, wrap her in his arms and lose himself in her. He longed to touch her, hold her, kiss her, make love to her.

Plain and simple, he wanted her. Bad. Even if he tried, his body refused to hide his need. The moment she stirred, she'd feel him. And there wasn't a thing he could do about it, short of getting out of this bed.

And damned if Rafe could force himself to move. Even if he should.

He could tick off a hundred reasons he shouldn't allow himself to give in to the urge. Sierra deserved a forever kind of man, a forever kind of love. The kind Noah had found with Lyssa. The kind her brother Mitch shared with his wife, Emily.

Not a man whose scars—both inside and out—made him damaged goods.

Rafe breathed in deep and slow, taking in every scent, every touch, burning the memory of the moment into his brain for the long, lonely nights to come. He'd never imagined he'd be this close to her. But here they were. Together. In a small room, in a small bed, with nowhere to go.

Every minute for the last forty-eight hours he'd hoped Sierra would reveal a flaw, something that would drag him down to earth, prove that the dreams she'd inspired since they'd met were unrealistic and impossible fantasies.

His prayers had gone unanswered. She was everything he'd imagined. Brilliant, resourceful, courageous, and passionate in her loyalty and love for her family.

He'd only identified two imperfections. She was Noah's sister, and the woman was the most stubborn and tenacious person he'd ever met. Rafe had practically had to sit on her since they'd arrived to keep her in this room, safe and sound.

Unable to go to a hospital for fear Archimedes would discover she had survived, he'd treated her wounds and located this out-of-the-way motel that would take cash only.

Two solid days had passed since the explosion. The wait was grinding on both of them, but they were stuck here until Noah caught Archimedes. Personally, Rafe hoped his best friend killed the murdering psycho.

Until then, Rafe was trapped. With a woman who challenged and attracted and intrigued him more than anyone since… Rafe shoved aside the comparison. He couldn't dwell on what he couldn't change. Only learn from it.

Sierra shifted on top of him. His entire body turned rigid. He fought back his shuddering response. Maybe she'd move off, and he could escape into the tiny bathroom for an ice-cold shower before she realized—

A small moan escaped her, a whimper. She trembled, her nails biting into his chest.

Oh, Sierra.

He glanced down at her face, the long lashes resting against shadowed eyes, frantic movement just beneath her eyelids. He recognized the signs.

Another nightmare.

She dug her nails deeper into his skin. "Please, no. Please don't."

Rafe wrapped his arms around her. "Shh," he whispered, rubbing her back, careful not to jar her injured shoulder. "You're safe."

Sierra shook her head and with a sleep-limp fist pummeled his chest. "Rafe!" she shouted. "Help me!"

"I'm here. I'm not letting you go." He cupped her cheeks, stroking the smooth skin. "Wake up, darlin'. Let me see those baby blues."

She squeezed them shut even tighter. Obstinate even in the midst of a nightmare.

"Come on, Sierra." She was entangled fiercely in a memory, and he tried to tell her it was only a dream. "He won't hurt you. Not ever again." His thumb traced the pale translucence of her skin. She'd been through so much.

Her eyelids snapped open, expression foggy with sleep.

"Good morning," he said, his voice gravelly and deep.

She blinked. She moved her leg slightly against his hip. Her eyes widened; her cheeks reddened.

The pulse at the base of her throat accelerated. Her pupils dilated.

She didn't move away. She pressed closer instead.

His heart leaped. The burn simmering inside his gut exploded. He shook with the effort to maintain control.

He couldn't look away. She'd captured him with her gaze. He held his breath.

"Rafe," she whispered. Her tongue dampened her lips.

"You should move." He cleared his throat. "Or I should."

She lifted her hand from the bare skin of his chest. She nodded in agreement, tossing a wave of disappointment and resignation through him.

He allowed his hands to fall back to the sheets. All for the best. But right now he had to get away from here. He needed that shower or to dunk himself into a tub of ice. "I think I'd better—"

"Don't," Sierra whispered, straddling his hips. "I don't want to think. I don't want to remember. I want what you've been promising me for the last two days."

Sierra sank into him, pressing her lips to his, demanding a response.

Rafe couldn't stop himself. He didn't want to. His heart racing, he shoved aside the doubts and let his body take over. With a groan, he wrapped Sierra in his arms, giving in. The world melted away. Heat and sweat and want and need overwhelmed them both.

But lingering, in the still small place deep inside, Rafe knew he was probably making the biggest mistake of his life.

Chapter One

Present Day, San Antonio, Texas

Nightmares weren't supposed to invade twice—not in the daytime, anyway.

That way-too-familiar, incessant, head-knocking throb thudded against Sierra Bradford's temples in time with her pulse. She didn't want to open her eyes, but ignoring the truth had never worked out well for her, so she squinted and *tried* to remember.

Her cheek pressed against the cool metal of a half-rusted floor. She attempted to raise her hand to ease the pounding in her head, but she couldn't move her arms. Thick rope cut into her wrists.

Her mind whirled in confusion. No. Archimedes was dead. He had been for over two months. This must be a nightmare. It wasn't real. It couldn't be.

"What was she doing with a gun? Who the hell is she?"

The man's harsh words skewered past the pounding at the back of Sierra's head. She twisted to identify the man to match the voice. All she could make out was a utility belt against a dark blue uniform. Her gut tightened. She followed her line of sight, and there it was. A badge. Before she could see his face, he turned his back and walked away. Military cut, dark hair. About five-ten, one seventy-five.

"Please. Don't hurt us."

A voice she recognized all too easily. The past couple of days careened through her mind. Her best friend's phone call asking for help. A few computer searches yielding more questions than answers.

Neither Sierra nor Mallory had expected to be stopped by the police and ambushed, though.

The sound of a vicious smack reverberated around her. Mallory cried out in pain. Desperate, Sierra struggled against her bindings and rolled to her back. Her gaze flashed through the corroded interior of an old van, landing on Mallory's terrified gaze. The corner of her mouth bled. Even worse, five-year-old Chloe clung to her mother, terror engraved on her face.

No way was Sierra letting anyone be kidnapped—especially not her goddaughter and best friend.

Okay, Sierra. Think.

Chloe whimpered, burying her head against her mother's side. Hands and feet bound, Mallory scooted her daughter behind her as best she could, away from the man looming over them, a bandanna hiding his face.

"Please," Mallory said, begging. "Let us go. We won't say anything. Chloe's just a little girl."

"We ain't letting no one go without the boss's say-so."

Sierra shifted just slightly. If she could only get enough leverage. With a shout, she bent her knee and rammed her foot as hard as she could against the guy's side. The force carried her back. She lost the follow-through.

He grunted and leaped at her. With a loud curse, he let loose and slugged her. Hard. The blow snapped Sierra's head against the van's metal floor. "Think you're smart, don't you?"

She blinked back the tears of pain. She wouldn't give these guys the satisfaction of knowing she could barely see after that last crack across her jaw.

He climbed on top of her. "I'll enjoy teaching you a lesson," he uttered, his fetid breath close to her ear, wrinkling her nose.

She stilled, staring into his nondescript brown eyes.

He slid the cold metal knife along her throat before tugging the weapon away. "Not so tough now, are you?" He nicked her, and warm blood trickled along her skin.

She stiffened. A wash of white noise enveloped the world, overwhelming her senses. She couldn't see. She couldn't hear. Nothing. Oh, God. Nothing.

Sierra fought to stay focused, fought the roar overwhelming her. She blinked, shaking her head against the terrifying, claustrophobic memory. The horrifyingly small closet. No escape. Trapped.

She couldn't lose herself. Mallory and Chloe needed her. She squeezed her eyes tight and silently recited a half dozen letters of the alphabet backward. The fog cleared a bit.

He checked the rope around her wrists and heaved her across the van's floor. "The boss'll want to talk to you."

"Judson, I didn't sign up for kidnapping a kid." A shaking voice filtered from the front of the van.

"Shut up, you idiot." Judson opened the back

of the van. "Get comfortable, you three. We're going for a one-way ride."

He chuckled and slammed the door shut. Sierra struggled to a seated position, moving closer to Mallory.

Who are they? she mouthed to Mallory. *Buddies of your ex? Would he go this far?*

Mallory blinked back tears. "I don't know," she whispered. "I thought he was setting me up at work, but this...?"

"No talking!" Judson shouted.

A slide and click echoed behind Sierra. He had a bullet in the chamber now. She'd recognize the sound of a Glock anywhere. Her brothers' favorite gun.

"Say another word and I won't wait for the boss."

"No!" Chloe screamed.

"Shh, Button," Mallory said. "We'll be okay."

"Keep her quiet or I gag you all."

Judson turned to the driver. "Get us out of here. Slow and steady until we're outside of San Antonio. We don't own *every* cop."

The engine roared to life. Over Chloe's head, Sierra met Mallory's gaze. They had one chance. Sierra's feet were still free. They couldn't stay in this van. If they did, she had no doubt they wouldn't make it out alive.

She edged toward the rear doors.

"Call the boss. Tell him we've got an extra passenger. He don't like surprises."

The van started forward. They were out of time.

Be ready, she mouthed to Mallory.

After Mallory's quick nod Sierra pressed herself against the side of the van. She wouldn't make the same mistake again. She needed the leverage, or they were all dead. She'd only have seconds to kick open the door before Judson killed her.

Tucking her legs, she aimed for the door and hit the lock with the heel of her boot. Once. Twice. The metal snapped. The door flew open.

"Come on!" Sierra rocketed out of the moving van, taking a roll, scraping her arm on the asphalt.

She looked up. Mallory struggled to nudge Chloe out with her body, but the girl didn't move. Desperation painted her mother's face.

"You can do it, Chloe," Mallory cried, squirming to the van's edge. "Jump."

The little girl shook her head. Fear froze her.

Sierra stumbled to her feet, racing toward the van. "Come on, Chloe!"

The van screeched to a halt. Mallory and Chloe tumbled backward.

"Go, Sierra!" Mallory yelled. "Run."

Sierra kept coming. She had to help them,

but the two men jumped from the van, their feet hitting the highway. They slammed the door closed. Mallory and Chloe were trapped.

If Sierra went back, they'd all be caught. A gunshot exploded into the night. A bullet struck near her feet, then a hot burn pierced her thigh. She had no choice. She zigzagged down the highway, away from her best friend, praying her movements would offer Mallory another chance to escape.

Veering to the side of the road, she dived into a patch of tall grass. Headlights flashed. A semi sounded its horn at the van blocking the road. The big truck slowed.

The van took off with a squeal of tires, its mud-covered license plate useless.

Sierra fought against the pain and stumbled back to the asphalt. She ran to the edge of the road yelling, praying the trucker would see her. He drove past. She sank to her knees, blood covering her right leg.

A hiss of brakes sounded, and the semi pulled over.

She looked up as a man ran toward her.

"Mallory. Chloe," she whispered. And passed out.

MERTZON, TEXAS, WASN'T on the way to any-where. Just the way Rafe Vargas liked it. He pulled his truck past the town's three restaurants. Each window had gone dark, a large Closed sign blinking the news. Sunday night. He should've known better than to think he'd find a restaurant open.

Rafe's stomach rumbled. After a day of training to keep his combat moves sharp, he'd been hankering for a greasy burger with onion rings. Nothing better at a small-town diner. Oh, well. Not as if he wasn't used to disappointment. He turned off toward the Mertzon Inn, a small hole-in-the-wall motel. He appreciated the location several blocks off Highway 67. Out of the way, not obvious.

He'd situated himself a couple hours from Carder, Texas, the headquarters for CTC. He liked working for Covert Technology Confidential. He liked helping people in trouble who had nowhere else to turn. He liked using the deadly skills Uncle Sam had drilled into him for the right reasons. But he also appreciated staying far enough away from headquarters that he didn't have to socialize much. Besides, lately many of his colleagues had found their soul mates. They were too damn content and satisfied. Not that he wasn't happy for them… and envious. But he didn't need the reminder of what might have been.

Of course there happened to be another reason to locate himself a good distance from an airport, be it CTC's private strip or a commercial facility. Rafe couldn't fly to Denver on a whim.

To see *her*, the biggest mistake of his life.

Sierra was *not* someone he should be thinking about. Not now. Not ever.

Rafe parked the car across from the motel, scanning the lot's perimeter. He'd stayed alive this long by being cautious, not doing the expected. This was his last night in Mertzon. He was getting too comfortable. Too recognizable. He'd move on tomorrow. Find another town, another motel. Another temporary home.

His first stop, to verify that the small slip of paper he'd inserted into the doorjamb earlier in the day hadn't been moved.

He probably could've used some of CTC's electronic toys, but sometimes low tech did the job better. And safer. No one could jam a paper's nonexistent, electronic signal.

His gaze slid above the Do Not Disturb sign. Still there. Good. He rounded the building. The motel's small office had hung out the Closed sign and locked the door. Evening church. Being in Mertzon was like going back in time fifty years. Rafe didn't mind. Fewer people; fewer questions.

Once he'd completed his surveillance, and

satisfied he hadn't been located, he unlocked his small room and snagged a can of Texas-style chili out of a paper bag sitting in the corner. His movements smooth with practice, he disengaged a can opener from his utility knife and punctured the top, then headed back outside. He rested his dinner on the truck's engine to heat up. Not exactly gourmet, but filling enough on an unusually warm January night.

Rafe pulled out a longneck bottle of beer from his ever-ready cooler and waited for his dinner to heat. He had this particular meal down to a science. At least he wasn't living on protein bars. Or worse.

The curtain fluttered in the window of the room next to his. Rafe set down the beer and tensed, his hand easing toward his weapon. He'd stayed alive by never making any assumptions.

Seconds later the door cracked open, and a small head peeked through the opening.

Rafe relaxed and settled back against the truck. "Hi, Charlie."

The seven-year-old boy looked down the row of doors one way, then the other, before tiptoeing out of the room, his eyes wide, staring at the chili bubbling on the engine.

"Whatcha doing, Mr. Vargas?"

"Fixing dinner. The diner's closed."

"Yeah, I know. Mama had to close up, then she went to clean the mayor's house. She won't be home until late." The boy's stomach growled.

"Wait here, Charlie," Rafe said. He paused, raking his gaze up and down the kid in speculation. "Don't go near the engine. It's hot."

Rafe strode back into the dingy motel room, with its Spartan furnishings. Digging into his supplies, he grabbed two spoons and a bowl.

The boy stood on his tiptoes peering at the chili, balanced precariously near the engine.

"Charlie," Rafe's voice warned, quiet so as not to startle the kid, but firm. "What did I tell you?"

He grimaced and scooted back. "I didn't know you could cook like this. When we lived in our car last summer, we ate cold stuff." He wrinkled his nose. "Cold peas don't taste good. They're mushy."

"Better than being hungry." Rafe snagged the chili with a napkin and poured half the meal into the bowl before handing it to Charlie.

"I guess," the boy said, stirring the meal. He couldn't quite take his eyes away from Rafe's face. "Why do you wear a patch?"

The words sped from his mouth as if he'd been warned not to ask the question but couldn't help himself.

Rafe blew on the chili and swallowed a bite. "Well, I got used to wearing it on the pirate ship…"

Charlie's eyes grew wide with shock. "Really?"

Rafe adjusted the eye covering. "Nah. I was in the war. I got hurt, and it messed up my eye. It's taking a long time to heal." That was the fairy-tale version, of course. Fifteen men had died during the operation that had damaged his eye. It might never heal completely, but Rafe considered himself lucky to make it out alive.

"Are you a hero?" Charlie asked.

"No."

"Oh." The boy stared down at his dinner.

Rafe had disappointed the kid, but what could he say? The truth was much too complicated, so Rafe settled for another bite of dinner. The mild heat didn't give him the kick he liked. He tapped in some Tabasco Habanero Sauce. Another bite. Now that was more like it. He glanced over at Charlie's rapt expression. "Want some?"

Charlie grinned and held out his bowl.

Rafe hesitated. "You sure?"

"Yeah."

Rafe dropped a smidgen onto the chili nestled in the boy's spoon. Charlie swallowed a big bite. Immediately he started coughing. His ears turned red; his eyes widened. Rafe bit his inner cheek to hide a rare grin. He patted Charlie on the back and handed him a cold bottle of water from the cooler.

The kid chugged it down. "I don't like that stuff," he squeaked, shoving the chili at Rafe.

"I think you got the worst of it." Rafe ignored the boy's outstretched hand. "It's safe. I promise."

With a suspicious gaze into the bowl, Charlie stuck out his tongue, swiping the meat and beans for a tentative taste. "It's okay."

"Eat up."

"Thanks, Mr. Vargas." Charlie downed half the bowl, then stared at the remainder. "I'll save the rest for Mama. Her boss wouldn't let her bring leftovers home tonight."

"Tell you what, Charlie. You finish your dinner. I've got enough for your mom."

The little boy grinned and ran back to his room. Charlie was a good kid. Rafe sighed. He just prayed the next few years gave Charlie and his mom a few breaks. Rafe knew from firsthand experience how easy it could be to go down the wrong path.

Charlie returned with a chocolate snack cake. "Today is January 31. I'm seven today, and Mama bought me a couple of cupcakes."

He tore one in two and handed it to Rafe. "This is for you."

"Thank you, Charlie." Rafe didn't know if he'd be able to choke down the cake, but Charlie's proud expression decided for him. "So, do you go for the frosting or the filling first?"

"Cake first." Charlie bit at the bottom of the dessert.

"I'm a filling man," Rafe said.

A few bites later the dessert was gone. "Your birthday, huh?" Rafe turned to his SUV and reached into the glove box. He pulled out a yo-yo and turned back to Charlie. "Happy birthday."

The boy reached out his hand and touched the toy with tentative fingers. "It's mine?"

"Someone gave me one when I was a little older than you." Rafe wedged his finger into the slipknot and executed a couple of throw downs. He went into a Sleeper, then Rock the Baby. "Now you try."

Rafe coached Charlie for a half an hour. A car rattled into the motel parking lot. Charlie looked over and bit his lip. "It's Mama. I'm not s'posed to leave the room."

A tired-looking woman exited the clunker vehicle. "Charlie Ripkin, exactly what do you think you're doing?"

"Look, Mama. Mr. Vargas gave me a birthday present."

She ruffled her son's hair. "Thank Mr. Vargas. You have to go to bed. School tomorrow."

Charlie walked over. "Thank you for the yo-yo. Can we play again tomorrow?"

"I don't know if I'll be around tomorrow, but you keep practicing. Here are some extra strings." Rafe tucked a hundred-dollar bill into the packet and placed it in Charlie's hand. "You might want to change the string before you play with it again."

The boy's grin widened. "Thanks, Mr. Vargas. This is the best birthday ever." Charlie gave Rafe a huge hug and disappeared into the motel room.

"I hope he didn't bother you, Mr. Vargas," Elena Ripkin said in an exhausted voice. She pushed her ash-colored hair away from her face.

Rafe took his card and wrote a phone number on the back. "I have a friend looking for help. It pays well. Give him a call. Use my name." He handed her a CTC card with his boss's name and number.

Elena's hand trembled when she clutched the bit of card stock. "Why? You don't even know me."

"I know enough," Rafe said. And he did.

The background check had revealed a woman whose husband had been killed in an oil field accident. Within months, she and Charlie had been evicted from their apartment. They'd lost everything.

A lot like Rafe's family. And their story had *not* had a happy ending.

If he could give Charlie some hope…maybe he wouldn't end up like Rafe's brother, Michael. Dead at seventeen on the streets of Houston, executed by a rival gang.

THE WIND SHOOK the rickety trailer. Mallory huddled in the corner of the small bedroom's makeshift cot, wrapping her arms around her daughter. Her heart still raced. Somehow she had to save them, but the trailer's window had been boarded up and the door locked from the outside. Mallory's fingers were bleeding from working at the thick planks of their prison. She let out a frustrated sigh. There was no escape.

At least the cowboy had untied them, even if Judson had cursed while the younger man removed the binding. It gave them a shot. She rubbed her wrists. The rope burns would heal. If they got out of here alive.

Mallory had no idea where they were. Far from San Antonio, though. They'd been locked in that van for hours, driving intermittently, occasionally stopping for Judson to make a phone call.

Whoever their kidnapper had contacted, it hadn't put him in a good mood.

"Mommy," Chloe whimpered, burrowing deeper into her mother's arms. "I want to go home. I want my kitty. Princess Buttercup will get scared if I'm not there."

With a gentle motion, Mallory hugged Chloe closer and kissed her head. "Hush, Button. Everything will be fine."

The door opened, and Judson stepped into the bedroom cradling a sawed-off shotgun in the crook of his arm. "It's not nice to lie to children."

Mallory pressed Chloe up against her, praying she could keep her daughter safe. "She's only a little girl. Please, let her go."

"That's the boss's decision. He wants to see you. Alone."

Mallory hesitated.

The man pointed his weapon toward Chloe. "I won't ask again."

Mallory kissed Chloe's forehead, then shifted to get up, but Chloe clutched at her arm, her tiny fingers digging into Mallory's skin in panicked desperation. "Mommy. Don't leave me. I'm sorry I didn't jump."

Chloe's face was streaked with tears. Mallory's heart breaking, she stroked her daughter's cheek, wiping away the dampness. She stood and fought to smile down at her daughter. "It's okay. Be brave. No matter what happens. I love you, Button. Always remember that."

Chloe whimpered, clinging to her mother.

Prying her daughter's fingers off her arm, and with one last kiss on Chloe's cheek, Mallory straightened and stepped away from the bed. "I'm ready."

Her captor smiled, his eyes cold and dead. "I doubt that. But if you tell the boss what he wants to know, he *might* be lenient."

She took one last look at Chloe, sent up a prayer and followed her captor through the narrow hallway into a living room. She glanced through the crack between the curtains at the front of the trailer. Night had fallen, but a bright spotlight illuminated the chaotic yard, strewed with trash and unidentifiable junk alongside several rusted-out car bodies. The place appeared abandoned, with a sea of darkness as far as the eye could see. No sign of civilization. No clue as to where they were.

A police car pulled up. The passenger-side window lowered.

"Judson. Get out here," a voice called.

"Damn," the guy muttered. He nodded at

the man at her side, his weapon resting in the crook of his arm. "Watch her."

Judson walked down the stairs. With tentative steps he approached the car. What kind of monster made a man who would kidnap a child that nervous?

One second later, a bullet slammed through Judson's head and he fell backward.

Mallory froze in horror. She turned her face away from the dead body. "Why?"

The cowboy turned to Mallory, his face grim. "Judson let your friend escape."

Did that mean Sierra was alive? *Please let her be alive. Please let her find us.*

The car door opened. The man beside her clutched his weapon with shaking hands. "Lady, if you want to stay alive, do exactly what he says and tell him what he wants to hear. If you don't, you and your kid won't make it out of here in one piece."

THE LONELY WHISTLE of a locomotive chugging through town pierced the night. Rafe handed Elena the last two cans of chili and directions to CTC before the exhausted women disappeared into her room.

Rafe locked his motel-room door and flopped onto the bed, not bothering to remove his boots.

He took a long swig of beer and flicked on the television.

Charlie didn't know it, but he'd given Rafe a gift. A welcome interruption. Because today would have been his fifth anniversary.

Except Gabriella had died a month before the wedding.

The mission had gone so wrong so fast. Gabriella had taken a spray of bullets. She'd had no chance. Because Rafe hadn't seen the betrayal coming. He hadn't protected her. He'd let emotions overrule his judgment.

It wouldn't happen again.

Rafe's knuckles whitened around the beer bottle. Never again.

Regret for what had happened would never leave him. He'd learned his lesson. A lesson he should've learned as a kid, but hadn't. A lesson he prayed Charlie would never have to learn. *Never let your heart rule your head. You'll get your head bashed in and your heart crushed.*

Words he lived by. Except for one night. With Sierra Bradford.

It had taken one kiss for him to forget the lessons of the past. He still couldn't believe he'd loved her, like he'd dreamed of from the moment he'd met her.

That one intimate encounter with Sierra had scared the hell out of him. He couldn't risk caring for her. Caring meant allowing his emotions to rule him once more. He couldn't do that. Sierra deserved someone who would give her everything. Heart, mind, body and soul. Not a man who not only didn't know how to be a part of a family but whose heart had been used up and destroyed.

Yeah, Sierra deserved someone whole, but that didn't stop him from dreaming about each kiss, every caress, or the way she'd held him tight against her as if she'd never let him go.

He dug into a pocket of his jeans and pulled out a small velvet pouch. He opened his hand, and a thin gold chain fell into his palm.

Sierra's. It had broken during their night together. A very passionate night he would never forget.

Don't go there. He tucked the chain back into his pocket.

He didn't need another night of dreaming about her.

He flipped channels, searching for another distraction. His cell phone rang. Blocked number. Hopefully a CTC job. No one else called him. "Vargas."

"It's Noah. I need your help."

It would have to be Noah. One of the few people he trusted. One of the few people who trusted Rafe. At least Noah would trust him until he found out Rafe had seduced his sister. And worse, run out on her. Even if it was for her own good.

Bracing himself, Rafe took a swig of beer. "What's up? I thought you hung up your spy suit."

Noah had been CTC's best of the best. Now he worked as a consultant, making cool gadgets to use in covert ops. He'd been almost as quixotic as Rafe—until he'd found someone to love him and a reason not to risk his life.

"Sierra's disappeared."

Chapter Two

Fighting the adrenaline rush, Rafe carefully set the bottle on the rickety nightstand. This wasn't happening. Not again. Right before Thanksgiving he'd searched for her. He'd barely gotten her out alive. He didn't like the twisting in his gut, the uncomfortable panic driving his heart to race.

"When did you last see her?" He fought to stay calm.

"A couple days ago. She left a cryptic message about not making it to Sunday lunch. She's been so reclusive since the attack, we gave her the space, but I went by her house to check on her. She's gone with at least one suitcase, bed unmade, dishes in the sink. That's not like her. I'm worried about her, Rafe. She hasn't been the same since—"

"Archimedes. Damn him." His teeth ground together. Good thing Archimedes was dead.

Rafe would have taken great satisfaction in killing the psycho for what he'd done to Sierra. "You tracked her cell phone?"

"She knows how to block her signal. Or someone else does. That's what I get for having a sister who's better than I am at electronics. Even if she doesn't believe it."

"Zane might be able to hone in on her location."

"He's at CTC headquarters. I don't want the boss thinking she's gone off the deep end." Noah hesitated. "I know we don't want her working for CTC, but when Ransom put her on indefinite leave after Archimedes—at our insistence, if you remember—the light went out of her eyes. We screwed up there."

Rafe adjusted the patch over his eye and rose from the bed. "No, we didn't. The job's too dangerous. She could get hurt. Or worse." He'd be damned if Sierra put her life on the line any longer. She'd almost died once. If anything happened to her...

Rafe grabbed his duffel from the top of the closet. "I'll find her, and I'll bring her home. Then it's your job to keep her there."

"Just make sure she's okay. She's not herself these days, Rafe. She can't sleep. She's got circles under her eyes. I don't want to lose my sister. You and I both know how the nightmares can take over your life."

Yeah, Rafe knew. He'd had his fair share. He also had up-close-and-personal experience with Sierra's demons. Her bad dreams had led to the best—and one of the worst—night of his life.

Spending time in Sierra's arms had made him want more. That's when he'd known he'd fallen way too deep. She'd ripped a hole in the Kevlar protecting his heart. She'd made him want forever. Except Rafe had learned all too well that love destroyed. He didn't matter, but he couldn't bear to hurt her more than he already had. So he'd walked away—for her sake—and instead had taken to watching her from afar. To make certain she was always safe.

She'd nearly caught him more than once, and he'd begged Ransom for another assignment. Something that would get her out of his constant thoughts. He'd believed he'd wanted distance, but he never should've ended his surveillance. If he hadn't, he'd know exactly where to find her. "Did you check the buses and airlines?"

"I'm working on it."

"I'll call when I find her." Rafe stuffed his 1911, a Bowie and his P-11 with its ankle holster in his bag, along with ammunition, a secure satellite phone and some of Noah's more interesting tracking devices.

Now all Rafe had to do was find her.

He tapped a few keystrokes into one device and started the search. He had a bad feeling. He didn't know if his gut was warning him of trouble or if he simply dreaded seeing Sierra again. Once he found her, could he resist her? Could he walk away again…and did he even want to try?

ILLUMINATED SIGNS DOWN the San Antonio street kept the road brightly lit even though night had fallen. The 18-wheeler's engine rumbled in idle. Sierra clutched the door handle and shoved it open.

"Thanks for the lift," she said, easing out of the truck.

"You sure you don't want me to take you to the hospital?" the driver asked.

When her foot hit the ground, a shot of pain pierced her thigh. She couldn't stop the wince.

"I'm fine." And doing a lot better than Mallory and Chloe. First she had to take care of her leg. She'd be no good finding them if she passed out and ended up in the ER. Gunshot wounds at the hospital meant cops. Cops meant trouble.

She forced a smile and turned to look up

at the man who'd saved her life when he'd stopped. She dragged the bag containing her laptop, extra money and credit card from the seat. She'd stashed it in the trunk when she and Mallory had left to pick up Chloe. Even though the car keys had vanished sometime during the abduction, luckily Sierra had been able to pop the trunk release just inside the driver's side door and retrieve her belongings. "Thanks again."

The diesel revved before the truck's horn blared and the vehicle rumbled down the road. Sierra walked away from the motel, limped down several long blocks and hurried as best she could across four lanes of traffic. If anyone asked the trucker about her, they wouldn't locate her easily.

After a quick stop at a convenience store for bandages, a burner phone and a few other supplies, she trudged another mile before locating the perfect, most nondescript motor inn on the street.

The place reminded her of another motel, another time. Another place.

She'd learned a lot from Rafe Vargas that week. Most lessons she preferred to forget. But how to disappear in plain sight, that was a skill she would find useful tonight.

Ready to collapse, she pushed through the

motel's office door, causing a dangling bell to chime. Within a few minutes, Sierra had laid down the last of her cash in exchange for a key. Once she'd locked herself inside the room, she sagged against the door.

She dumped the medical supplies on the rickety table and unbuttoned her jeans. She slipped them over her hips. The material stuck against her thigh. She hissed and froze. The blood had dried.

Closing her eyes, she slowly, gingerly tugged the denim away from her wound.

A sharp burn sliced up and down her leg. She whimpered. Maybe she should just rip it off, like a stuck bandage.

"One, two, three—"

A quick tug and the pants dropped to the floor. Sierra's knees gave out. She sank to the floor, biting down hard on her lip to keep from screaming.

That hurt. Bad.

Her thigh throbbed, blood dripped from the reopened wound. For a moment she simply sat on the floor, rocking back and forth. When the spots stopped spinning in front of her eyes, she stood on shaky legs and padded to the bathroom.

Propping herself against the wall, Sierra irrigated the wound with hot water, picking out denim fibers and dirt, stopping every so often to lean her head against the wall and suck in several deep breaths before starting again.

A pounding knock sounded at the door.

Sierra limped to the table, wishing the kidnappers hadn't taken her gun, and grabbed the scissors she'd purchased. As fast as she could, she crossed the room and slipped behind the door, knuckles white, her teeth biting into her lip.

"Mrs. Jones?"

The motel manager's voice called through the door. He knocked again.

She said nothing. Surely he'd go away.

Her thigh throbbed in time with her pulse. She could hear every breath. She waited. After a minute or two, her muscles relaxed.

Urgent whispers filtered through the door, but she couldn't make out the words. The doorknob jiggled. Metal on metal scraped. Damn. No one knew she was here. Had the men who kidnapped Mallory and Chloe found her?

Sierra skirted into the bathroom, gripping the scissors even tighter. If someone came in, she wanted a good look at him before she attacked.

"Mrs. Jones?"

Silent, Sierra peeked between the crack of

the bathroom door just below the hinge. She made out the manager's stout figure first.

The man frowned at the towels and trash scattered around the room. "She's not here," he said. "You'll have to come back."

The door creaked. "I'm her husband."

She clutched the doorknob with a death hold. She'd recognize that voice anywhere, the deep rumble, the smooth velvet baritone, but she couldn't believe those three words had escaped his lips.

"Rafe?" Sierra nearly rushed into the room before she stopped herself. Parading around in her underwear wasn't an option. She peeked around the door.

"Hi, honey," Rafe said, his expression grim, his voice soft and deadly. "I'm home."

Before Sierra could contemplate how he'd found her, Rafe shunted the manager out of the room with an excuse, grabbed a bloodstained towel from the floor and wrenched open the bathroom door. He shoved the cloth at her. "What the hell is this?"

She snapped a clean bath towel from a rod and wrapped it around her waist to hide her high-cut panties and naked legs. "What are you doing here?"

"That's a bullet graze," he said, ignoring the question. He tugged the terry cloth back to reveal her injury, and before she could say a word, swept her into his arms. Gently, carefully he laid her on the small bed.

He straightened and tossed his Stetson on the chair beside the table.

With his six feet four inches of pure muscle and outlawesque eye patch, he looked like a hero who'd walked straight out of a romance novel. He'd certainly featured in more than one of her own fantasies. At least until the morning after one very passionate night. She'd dropped her guard, flayed open her heart and he'd stomped all over it.

"I don't need the help. I've got the situation under control." She propped herself up on her elbows and tried to shift to the other side of the bed.

He grasped her arm and held her in place, pushing aside the towel. He didn't speak, but probed at the angry skin surrounding the wound, then arched his brow as he met her gaze.

Sierra squirmed under his lingering, enigmatic look. Rafe shook his head and rummaged through the supplies. He returned to her side with antiseptic, bandages, antibiotic ointment and tape.

He straightened her leg and held her down with a firm hand. "Let me do this. I've had a lot of practice." He tilted the antiseptic onto a large gauze square. "Brace yourself," he said, and dabbed at the flesh.

She sucked in a sharp breath. Her leg jerked.

"Easy does it." He bent over the wound and blew, easing the sharp sting.

Sierra glanced away, her cheeks burning as he poked and prodded close the top of her thigh. He was nothing but professional, even distant. In fact he'd acted as if it were nothing but business as usual.

They hadn't seen each other since a very awkward Thanksgiving dinner at her father's house the week after he'd rescued her.

One look and her heart had leaped at the memory of the way he'd touched her, the way he'd driven away her nightmares. At least for a few hours.

Until he'd vanished from their bed. And then walked away without a word after the family gathering he clearly had only attended to out the fact that she worked for CTC to her family. Noah in particular.

Sierra's dreams had returned with a vengeance. Rafe hadn't come back. A time or two she'd imagined she'd recognized him in a crowd, that he'd found her, that she'd been more than a convenient and willing night of passion, that he hadn't simply used her.

She'd been wrong. A second glance and the imaginary figure had vanished. So had the rose-colored glasses.

How had she allowed herself to be duped? That she'd trusted a man who could so easily walk away.

Well, she wouldn't allow herself to be seduced again. By his memory, by her fantasies. She couldn't trust him. Not with her heart. She'd learned her lesson. And she was an excellent student.

He pressed the final strip of tape against her skin but didn't move his tan hand from her thigh. A tingling of awareness rose across her skin, settling deep in her belly.

Now if she could just convince her body to listen to her mind.

Rafe simply looked at her, the muscle in his jaw pulsing, holding her gaze hostage.

Despite her decision and best of intentions, she couldn't control her response to his closeness. Being in her underwear on the receiving end of Rafe Vargas's hot stare was a bad place to be. The man could still make her heart flip-flop. Even when he was obviously furious, like now.

She blinked, breaking the spell, and quickly tossed the bedspread over her naked legs.

Only one way to handle him. Get on the offensive and don't back down. "In what fantasyland are you my husband?"

IF THE MOTEL owner hadn't been so damn protective of Sierra's room number, Rafe wouldn't have had to resort to the lie. He wasn't about to dwell on why the statement had crossed his lips all too easily, nor was he willing to apologize for it.

He'd dreamed of having Sierra in his bed for the past two months. His hand stroked the bandage on her thigh gently. But not like this. Never like this. When Rafe had first entered the room and had seen that bloody towel on the floor, his knees had nearly buckled.

A few inches and the bullet would've nicked her femoral artery. She'd have bled out.

She'd come too damn close to dying. Twice.

But she was alive. And mostly well. She lay propped up on the bed, shadows beneath her eyes, her cheeks pale. He cataloged the injuries he could see: the scrapes, the bruise darkening her jaw and cheekbone. She must be black-and-blue.

Someone needed to pay.

At his silence, a flash of blue fire erupted in her eyes. He'd witnessed the flame more than once: usually when someone crossed her, but also when she'd wrapped her arms and legs around him.

Her very presence drew him in. The small motel room's walls closed in on him. He had to let the past go.

Every instinct inside him fought the urge to wrap his arms around her, breathe in her scent and just hold her close. If he closed his eyes, he knew he could feel the silk of her skin beneath him, smell the clean scent of her hair, remember her generosity as he held her, giving him her heart and soul.

And he'd been stupid—or smart enough— to throw it away when all he'd wanted was to stay with her.

He'd done the right thing. He had to believe that. The alternative—well, he just wouldn't consider the alternative.

Instead of acting on his urges, he cocked his head to the side. "What am I doing here? Oh, no reason. I get a call from Noah that you'd vanished from Denver without telling your family only months after being held captive by a serial killer. And then, after you use your debit card at a convenience store, I find you a mile away in a barely up-to-code motel room, shot and obviously assaulted. I don't know, Sierra. Why don't you guess what I'm doing here? Saving you one more time."

"A mile would've been far enough if any-one but you had been searching," she mut-tered under her breath. Her lips flattened in a straight line. "Go home, Rafe. And tell Noah if he wants to send a babysitter, pick someone else."

The words, though expected, still hurt. No distance would ever be far enough if she was in trouble. "Tough. You got me. And I'm not budging." He lifted his hand and hovered over the stark mottling on her face. "Honey, who did this to you?"

Her eyes glistened and she looked away. "Don't be nice. I can't take it."

"What are you involved in?" He leaned closer and with gentle fingers clasped her chin, forc-ing her gaze to meet his. "An op?"

"You and Noah got me suspended, remem-ber?"

"And if I remember correctly, you seem to find ways to insert yourself into places you shouldn't be."

"The Kazakhstan situation was different. Zane needed help. He just didn't know it yet," Sierra countered. "I found the link between the terrorists and that charity, didn't I?"

"Not the point. I'm not saying you're not good at your job. Hell, you're the best. We all know that."

Her mouth dropped open, but instead of coming back at him like Rafe had expected, she gripped the sheets, twisting the fabric. "I might be good at the keyboard, but not in the field. I screwed up. I should've stopped it."

Her eyes shifted away from his gaze. She seemed to be struggling for words. Finally a sharp curse escaped her. "I want more than anything to kick you out of this room and tell you and Noah to shove your concern where the sun doesn't shine."

"Sierra—"

"But I can't." She lifted her chin and met his gaze, direct, unwavering. "I bought a burner phone to call Ransom. I need CTC's help, Rafe. Someone kidnapped my best friend and her daughter. My goddaughter." She paused, pain slicing over her features. "I let it happen, and I need you to help me save them."

MALLORY COULDN'T STOP staring at the blood seeping from the dead man's body. Her insides went cold. She glanced back at the trailer. She had to get Chloe out of here, but how?

"Get rid of the body," the voice from the passenger side of the police car snapped. "And bring the girl here."

"Yes, boss," her guard said.

"No. Please." Mallory would say anything, promise anything, to keep her daughter safe.

Two men picked up Judson and carried him to the side of the trailer. Mallory's captor disappeared inside, leaving her alone.

Every instinct screamed to run.

A tall man opened the car door and stood. He wore a cop's uniform. There was a touch of gray at his temples; his eyes were obscured by sunglasses.

"I wouldn't advise trying to escape, Mrs. Harrigan. Or your daughter will pay the price."

The aluminum door fluttered closed.

"Mommy! Don't leave me anymore. I was scared."

Chloe pulled at the cowboy's arm.

"Let her go," the cop ordered.

Within seconds Chloe raced to her mother. Mallory lifted her little girl into her arms and hugged her tight. She looked over her daughter's shoulder. "Please let her go. She's only five."

"Chloe, do you want to leave?" the police officer asked.

The little girl nodded against her mother's shoulder. "Princess Buttercup needs me. She has to eat her dinner. Kitties can't miss dinner, you know. You have to take good care of them."

The man smiled, a grin that made Mallory's stomach roil.

"I'll bring your cat to you, Chloe, but only if you tell me something very important."

Chloe bit her lip. "I don't know anything 'portant."

"I imagine you do. Look at me."

Twisting in Mallory's arms, her daughter stared at the man. He stroked his chin. "What's the name of the woman who tried to help you escape from the van?"

Mallory tightened her hold on her daughter.

"You're squishing me, Mommy. Not so tight." She wiggled and stared hard at the cop's chest. "You have a shiny badge, so you're not a stranger, but why do you want to know about Sierra? I saw her fall. Is she okay?"

With a silent groan, Mallory closed her eyes.

The cop smiled. "An unusual name. Perhaps your mother would be willing to tell us her friend's last name."

Chloe nodded. "Mommy knows it. I know it too. Just like my name is Chloe Harrigan. Sierra's name is Sierra Bradford."

The man nodded at his driver. "You get that?"

"Yes, sir." Within seconds he'd placed a call.

Mallory's hope sank. Now that her daughter had inadvertently put a target on Sierra's back, how would her best friend ever be able to find them? She bit her lip, her mind whirling. She was on her own. How could she save them?

The cop crossed his arms in front of him, his smirk too satisfied. "Thank you for the information, Chloe. You've been a lot of help."

"Where's Princess Buttercup?" Chloe asked with a pout. "You promised."

"And I always keep my promises," he said. "Eventually. Right now, Glen will take you to your room. Your mother and I are going to have a little…chat."

Leaning her forehead against her daughter's hair, Mallory tried not to tremble.

Glen tugged Chloe from her mother's arms. "Mommy!"

The cop grabbed Mallory's arm. Hard. She had no idea why they'd taken her, but she was afraid she'd soon find out.

"I have a few questions for you, Mrs. Harrigan. If I hear what I want, maybe your daughter won't have to watch her mother die."

Chapter Three

The stillness in the motel room made Sierra want to squirm. She sat perched on the edge of the bed, back stiff. She'd filled Rafe in on the van, the kidnapping, everything.

How Mallory had called her after discovering missing money at her job for the San Antonio Rodeo. How Sierra had followed the money trail by digging into a few files and discovering numbers that had been adjusted after Mallory had reconciled her books. How they'd both wondered if her ex's threats about their custody battle might be related. How that routine traffic stop on the way to pick up Chloe from school had led to the abduction and her getting shot. No point in sugarcoating the truth.

Of course, in typical Rafe fashion, he hadn't said a word. The muscle in his jaw pulsed erratically, and he just stared. Stone-faced and silent.

His unblinking gaze bored into her. Uh-oh. She recognized the expression and forced herself not to look away. Rafe might be an enigma to practically everyone, but she knew a few things about him. He maintained control 99 percent of the time. She'd only seen him lose it once: their night together. One he obviously regretted—as did she.

Sierra still couldn't believe Noah had sent Rafe, of all people, to find her. Okay, maybe she could believe it. Rafe was one of the few people Noah really trusted—outside family. Still, she would have preferred to face almost anyone else from CTC.

Her discomfort didn't matter, though. She'd had no choice but to ask for his help. Mallory and Chloe couldn't wait. They needed rescuing.

And damn him, Rafe was the very best. CTC called on him when the job was too complicated, too dangerous and required no nerves and even less fear.

And now, *she* needed him.

With a shaky hand she pushed back her hair over her ear. He was full-on quiet, which meant he didn't want to speak whatever was on his mind. A waft of the antiseptic he'd used still burned. She wrinkled her nose. She hated the odor. At twelve she'd spent every afternoon at the hospital during her mother's final illness.

That scent did more than make her gut ache, it made her heart hurt. She'd been unable to do anything to prevent her mother's death. Sierra could do something now...if Mallory and Chloe were still alive.

No. She wouldn't let herself even consider they weren't okay. Maybe frightened, but they had to be okay.

"I can't believe you've been kidnapped twice in two months," Rafe finally muttered with a shake of his head.

"Old news that's irrelevant," Sierra said. "And it's *almost* kidnapped. If Chloe hadn't been so scared—"

"You'd all be dead." Rafe crossed his arms. "This is how it's going to play. First, I'm calling Noah. He'll send a plane to take you back to Denver—"

"Not happening," she interrupted. No way was he pushing her out. She had to make things right. "Not until we find Mallory and Chloe."

"Sierra—"

"I'm a witness. I know them. You need me."

"Do you know who kidnapped them?"

She frowned. "They wore masks—"

"Do you have any suspects?"

He rubbed in the obvious with each question. She didn't have much to go on. "Mallory is getting ready to file paperwork to get full custody. Her ex has been fighting her—"

"Most abductions are committed by someone who knows the victim." Rafe stroked the stubble on his chin. "He involved other people, though, and that means loose ends. What does he get out of it, unless he plans to keep them prisoner? Or worse."

An icy chill settled in Sierra's gut. "The only other lead I have is that she discovered missing money at her job at the rodeo. I looked through some files Mallory brought home with her. I found a few suspicious entries, but I don't have anything solid. To be sure, I need a look at the accounting system."

"We need a warrant to do that. CTC has a contact on the San Antonio police force—"

She shook her head. "No cops. At least one helped with the kidnapping. I can't risk word getting out."

CTC had dealt with corrupt cops before. It's one of the reasons the company existed—when law enforcement couldn't or wouldn't help. Her father hated that about her career. He'd been a cop until a gunshot wound had put him in a wheelchair, but just because he was no longer on the force didn't mean you took the cop out of the man.

Rafe shook his head. "I can't promise anything but to be discreet—"

She opened her mouth to argue, but he placed his finger against her lips. "I'll call Ransom and request getting Zane out here. He's got the computer skills. We'll find your friend, but you *are* going back to Denver. We can handle this. Let me do my job."

"And you need to let me do mine." With a jerk, Sierra flung his hand away and swiveled to the opposite side of the mattress from Rafe. She stalked around the bed and picked up her soiled jeans from the floor. She didn't look forward to putting them on, but she had nothing else to wear. "I'm staying until we find Mallory and Chloe. If all you're going to do is put roadblocks in front of me, just go home. I'll contact Ransom myself and get someone else to help me." She snatched her burner phone from the table. "Mallory and Chloe don't have any more time. We've wasted too much debating already. I don't need your protection, Rafe. I need your help."

Rafe rubbed his temple. "You are so damn stubborn. Fine. I'm in."

Without a word he stalked out of the motel room, returning in moments with a duffel. He dropped it on the bed, unzipped it and threw a pair of sweatpants and a T-shirt at her. "Put them on. At least they're clean."

Catching the clothes, she nodded. "Fine."

Okay, that had been easier than she'd expected.

Surprised he'd given in, Sierra vanished into the bathroom, secretly relieved she wouldn't have to pull her jeans up over her wound.

She stepped into the huge sweatpants and slid them over her hips. After tightening the drawstring so they wouldn't fall off, she slipped on the T-shirt that fell to her midthighs despite her five feet ten inches. Rafe's clothes dwarfed her, but they would do.

Raising her chin, she stared into the mirror. "Are you sure you're up to this? Maybe Rafe and Noah are right," she said to the stranger looking back at her, scared, uncertain, despite her bravado in the other room.

No wonder Rafe was skeptical. Look at her. Circles under her eyes. Scrapes on her forehead, bruises darkening her cheek and chin. Where was the strong woman she'd always imagined herself to be? The one who could give all three of her brothers a run.

She knew the answer even if she didn't want to admit it. Archimedes had ripped something from deep inside her soul. She pulled the neck of the T-shirt lower. The infinity symbol he'd carved into her flesh glared at her, red and angry. A sign of how helpless she'd been in that small room. Completely at his mercy.

He'd gotten the drop on her then, just like the kidnappers had today. Despite her skills at the keyboard, Sierra hadn't reacted like an agent. Then or now.

But she knew in her gut she could help. Those accounts had made the back of her neck tingle. There was *something* hidden just beneath the surface. She could feel it.

"So, why didn't you see the trouble coming? Again?"

She adjusted the soft fabric to cover the scar, bent over the sink and slapped some water on her face. Rafe had instincts. But so did she. "You've followed your gut a million times. Numbers don't lie."

Right. But this case was more personal than anything she'd ever investigated. "Get a grip, Sierra." Mallory and Chloe couldn't afford for Sierra not to be on her A game.

Neither could Rafe. He needed a partner he could count on.

She gripped the edge of the bathroom sink. "You can do this," she lectured the shadow of herself. "For them."

THE BATHROOM DOOR had remained closed for too long. What was Sierra doing in there?

Rafe rubbed his hands over his face. What the hell was he going to do with her? She'd been through so much, but she'd fought like hell because her friend Mallory was in trouble. He admired the loyalty. He shouldn't have expected anything less from Noah's sister. But he could also see beneath the bravado, and the anger. Even the strongest could crack under enough pressure. Sierra loved fiercely. But that emotion could boomerang. Rafe should know.

He slipped his secure phone from his pocket and dialed a number. He needed facts, not feelings.

"I don't have another job for you, Rafe." Ransom didn't mince words when he answered. "Not yet."

Rafe grabbed his duffel and walked outside. "That's not why I'm calling. I need information from the San Antonio Police Department, and I need it hush-hush."

"What the hell's going on?"

"We may have some dirty cops. How far do you trust Cade Foster?" Rafe stuffed his belongings behind the seat in his truck.

"If I could tempt him to leave the San Antonio PD, I'd hire him in a heartbeat."

"Then I need everything you can find on Mallory Harrigan. For a new case." After a quick glance around, he filled in Ransom on what he knew of Sierra's friend, but he didn't mention Noah's sister. Not yet.

"I'll get back to you," Ransom said. "Does this have anything to do with Sierra Bradford flying down there a few days ago?"

Rafe nearly dropped the phone. "How did you know?"

"The same way I know you've been holed up in Mertzon," Ransom said. "It's my job to worry about my team." He ended the call.

Sometimes Ransom Grainger could be damned scary. It made the guy the best—and the worst—to work for.

Rafe strode back into the motel room. Sierra hadn't emerged. He paced back and forth a couple of times. He glanced at the bathroom door. No movement and no way around it. He had another call to make. He tapped in a very familiar number and let it ring.

Once, twice. His grip tightened. Maybe he'd luck out.

"Did you find her?" Noah snapped through the phone.

Or maybe not. "She's okay." Rafe winced at the half-truth.

A long silence settled through the phone until a sharp curse escaped his friend.

"What aren't you telling me?" Noah asked. "What's wrong?"

"Have you got a radar for trouble or something?" Rafe rubbed the bridge of his nose and repositioned his patch.

"When it comes to my family, you bet. Spill it, Vargas. What's going on with my sister?" Worry laced Noah's voice. "She's safe, isn't she?"

How was Rafe supposed to answer that? Noah wouldn't be put off, so Rafe relayed the situation. He kept a few details to himself. No need to tell big brother everything.

"You're taking the case," Noah said. "Good. And Sierra's coming home?"

Rafe didn't answer.

"Tell me you're putting her on the plane first thing tomorrow."

Rafe shoved his fingers through his hair. "She won't leave. Not until we find Mallory and Chloe. She blames herself."

Noah let out a sharp curse. "You can't convince her?"

"How easy is it to change a Bradford's mind about anything?" Rafe asked.

"Point."

"Besides she's got the skills. You know that." Rafe could deal with the ex, but if Mallory had been kidnapped because of the money, he could very well need Sierra's expertise to save the woman and her child.

Noah let out a long sigh. "Well, if she's going to jump into the deep end, I can't think of a better man to watch over her than you."

Rafe winced. If only Noah knew.

"Keep her safe. The family can't lose her. Dad's had enough hits the past few years."

"I'll do whatever it takes to protect her, Noah. I promise you that."

With a quick tap on the screen, Rafe ended the call. He paced the floor several times before hovering outside the small bathroom. Resigned to the reality of the situation, even if he didn't like it, he tapped gently. "You okay in there?"

A bang followed by a curse erupted from inside. "I'd be better if you weren't so big."

A corner of Rafe's mouth tilted up, but before he could respond his phone vibrated. He glanced at the screen and moved to the other side of the room. "What do you have, boss?" he asked in a low voice.

Ransom rattled off a series of facts. With each one, Rafe's frown deepened. What the hell was going on?

"You're sure about this?" Sierra wasn't going to be happy about the news. Or how he'd acquired his information.

"I'll let you know what I hear. Cade's keeping his ear to the ground," Ransom said.

Rafe pocketed his phone just as Sierra walked

out of the bathroom. He bit his cheek. "The clothes look good on you even though you're swimming in them."

"I've been thinking," she said, ignoring his comment and all business. "Her ex, Bud, had access to Mallory's house. He could've seen the files she brought home. He knows where Chloe goes to school, and the route Mallory takes."

"That gives him means and opportunity. The motive still feels fuzzy. What's his endgame?"

"I don't know." She grunted in disgust. "I got nothing."

"We're just getting started." Noting her uneven gait, Rafe dug into his duffel and passed a few ibuprofen and a bottle of water to her. "You're going to need it." For more reasons than one.

Sierra took a sip and swallowed the pills. "Thanks."

Rafe sucked in a deep breath. "I just got off the phone with Ransom. He has a connection with the San Antonio police—"

"You promised." She elbowed past him and stuffed the items she'd purchased into a plastic bag. "What have you done?"

"What I had to do," Rafe said, clasping her shoulders and turning her to face him. "Ransom trusts Cade. I trust Ransom. The question is, do you trust *us*?"

For a moment she didn't speak. Her gaze lowered, and Rafe let out a long, slow breath. "I see."

"It's not about you and Ransom," she said. "The kidnapper implied there was more than one cop involved. Why did you take the risk? What if word gets back to the kidnappers?"

"I've been running ops for over a decade. Accurate and complete information is the difference between failure and success." Rafe met her gaze. "Do you *trust* me, Sierra?"

She shrugged out of his grip. "I have no reason not to. Ransom counts on you. Noah believes in you." She paused. "I trust your ability to do this job."

The job. And nothing else.

The words remained unspoken, but Rafe received the message loud and clear. He didn't blame her. "Fair enough. But you *have* to trust me. Just like I have to trust you if we're going to be partners."

"That's good for a start, but I want more," Sierra said. "Keep me in the loop. No secrets. No lies. I deserve honesty from you."

She stood only inches from him and cocked her head. She didn't back down. One of her qualities Rafe truly admired.

He stretched out his hand. "Agreed."

She shook his hand. "Partners. So, what did

Ransom say? And don't give me that look. I recognize Noah's I-don't-want-to-tell-you-what-you-don't-want-to-hear look."

"Sit down and rest your leg," Rafe said. "We have a wrinkle."

After she settled on the bed, he pulled up a chair beside her. "From what you told me, the smart move would be to keep quiet about the abduction and find and eliminate the only witness—you. But this afternoon, before she and Chloe were abducted, your friend's boss called the cops and reported missing money. Tens of thousands."

She frowned at him. "I don't understand."

"The call shined a light on Mallory. When they searched her house, the place appeared as if someone had left in a hurry. You friend looks guilty as hell. Their working theory is she embezzled the money and skipped town, leaving her car on the side of the road."

Sierra shook her head. "It doesn't make sense."

"It does if that was the plan in the first place."

Rafe let his comments sink in.

Her eyes widened. "No. No way. This isn't some elaborate setup. Mallory would never do that."

"It's smart. It gives her time to disappear."

"She'd have to know I would never stop looking for her. Unless…" Sierra's voice trailed off. "Unless I was in on it."

"If that were the case, you wouldn't have asked for my help. I trust you, Sierra, but that doesn't mean I trust Mallory."

"She wouldn't. If you can't believe in her—"

"We have to explore every possibility," he interrupted. "And you have to bury your emotions. I admire your faith, but sometimes the people closest to us aren't what they seem." He placed his hand on hers and squeezed. "If you believe in her, convince me with facts, not feelings."

Sierra took a deep breath and nodded. "Mallory and I have known each other since we were eight years old, but she fell for the wrong guy when she was eighteen and got in over her head. She learned her lesson. She turned her life around. Besides, she loves her daughter more than anything. She would never do *anything* that would put Chloe in danger."

"Love and honor don't necessarily come together in a package. That love for her daughter could be the reason she betrayed you and took the money." He ran his thumb over her palm. "Some aren't strong enough to resist temptation even when they know it's wrong."

He gave her a pointed look and could see in her eyes she knew exactly what he meant. Heat rose into her cheeks. "We were discussing Mallory, not our mistake."

"Mistake. Definitely." Rafe let her hand go and put a few feet between them. "Okay. She's misunderstood and made some bad decisions. I've made my share, so I'll buy your argument. But now she's gone through a messy divorce. Her ex wants custody. According to Ransom, her credit is shot and she just received a huge deposit—received in cash by the way—into her bank account—"

"I knew about her credit, but she wouldn't take thousands of dollars. That's not possible."

"And these are the facts. *Fifty* grand," Rafe added. "It seems you *don't* know everything."

"Neither do you. Someone's framing her. Mallory *told* me money was missing from an account at the rodeo. She knows I'm a forensic accountant. So, of course she'd come to me. She trusted me to help her." Sierra lifted her chin. "Take me to Mallory's house. You want facts? I've got proof Mallory couldn't have left on her own or planned this."

"What are you talking about?"

"Princess Buttercup."

SWEAT BEADED ON Rafe's forehead. And not just from the unseasonably warm January. Even in the dead of night, the interior of the vehicle had heated up.

But Sierra Bradford was the reason the man who most of CTC knew as an unemotional iceman was sweating.

Damn, she was something else. She did everything with passion, and he really loved… no strike that. He *liked* that about her. She'd refused to back down for Mallory Harrigan. He respected the fight in her. Even if he could see the inevitable problems staring him in the face.

As to other passions…he pulled at the collar of his T-shirt. He should just stuff those memories into a cold shower as soon as possible.

With long-practiced discipline, he pulled himself out of the past. "I'll admit the cop's version of your friend's story is easy."

"Too easy," Sierra said.

"Probably." From Rafe's experience, nothing tied up that neatly, but answers weren't always a huge conspiracy either, though CTC ops tended to be more complicated than most.

He turned the vehicle onto the street heading toward Mallory's house. "I can't believe we're breaking and entering into a crime scene because your friend didn't take her cat."

"What's the big deal? Like you can't pick a lock at least as fast as my brother? I've read enough of your op reports to know exactly how far you'll go to get the job done, Rafe."

"I usually make nice with local authorities even if I'm lying… I don't go antagonizing them. Makes it hard to talk our way out of jail if we get caught," he countered.

"Princess Buttercup is Chloe's cat. That little girl loves her pet. Though I gotta admit, she's a spooky thing. She listens." Sierra sent a side-glance toward Rafe. "Besides, if she's there it's a fact in my favor. If she's in that house, Mallory didn't run."

"It's just a cat."

"Didn't you ever have a pet growing up?"

He shrugged. "No. We…moved around too much." Rafe's face closed off. Not that any of the hellholes his first—and worst—foster father had dragged him to would have been a safe place for a pet. It hadn't been safe for him or his brother. "Probably gets underfoot," Rafe said.

"Just wait until you meet her. If you don't like Princess Buttercup, you don't have a heart."

"I never claimed to." A bitter smile etched on Rafe's face. "I thought you knew that."

Sierra crossed her arms. "I'm not taking the bait, Rafe. I've read your ops reports. You may walk away from everything, but you care or you wouldn't do what you do." Sierra leaned forward. "Mallory's house is just around this bend."

The neighborhood was old, but well kept, and in line with Mallory's salary. Rafe pulled the truck to the curb a half block away from the house. Only a van sat parked in front of the house. Yellow tape barred the front entrance. "You recognize the vehicle?"

"It's not Mallory's. Or Bud's," she said, unclipping her seat belt. "I expected more people here."

"They don't believe anyone's in imminent danger," Rafe said. "They think she ran. They probably grabbed her computer equipment and left."

"They're wrong." She gripped Rafe's arm. "Can't you give us the benefit of the doubt? Just for a while."

"I am," Rafe said. "If I weren't, you'd be on your way to Denver." He paused. "You have your weapon?"

She shook her head. "The kidnappers took it."

Rafe pulled a gun from his duffel and handed it to her. "Take it. Use it if you need it. I have several."

"Always prepared?" she asked.

"I'm no Boy Scout, but I believe in the motto."

Sierra turned the gun in her palm, holding it with ease. Ransom wouldn't let anyone on the team without good firearm training. She tucked the weapon in her bag.

Rafe eased open the door of his truck. "Just wait here…and be on alert."

He exited the vehicle, his stride quiet and cat-like, ultra-aware. He scouted out several hiding spots behind the shrubbery surrounding the house, constantly glancing back at the car where she waited.

Everything was quiet. Too quiet.

Rafe walked around the truck, but Sierra had slipped out before he opened the door.

"How are you feeling?" he asked, cupping her elbow. "Dizzy, headache?"

"Just worried."

Sierra didn't have a poker face. She grimaced with each step. She needed rest. They'd grab the damned cat, and he'd put her to bed. "What do you know about Mallory's ex?" he asked, trying to distract her, and himself from where his mind had wandered. Sierra…in his bed. Alone.

"Bud," Sierra grimaced again, looking over the hood of the truck. "Not my favorite person. Mallory hid the truth from me for a long time, but I should've known. She refused to let me come visit the last couple of years, instead bringing Chloe to meet me halfway in Dallas.

The last time she wore heavy makeup, but I could see the bruises."

"No one wants to admit they can't handle their life. Did he hurt his daughter, too?"

"Once. Chloe got between them. It's why Mallory finally left."

He led her to the side of the house. "No reason to beg questions from the neighbors," he whispered. "We have three options with him. He created this elaborate ruse to kidnap the two of them, which seems unlikely. Mallory and Bud are working together, which also seems unlikely unless he's extorting her. Or, he's framing Mallory because a great way to get custody is to put your ex-wife in jail. Does he want his daughter that much?"

"He wants to hurt Mallory that much."

Rafe scanned the side yard carefully. No strange movements. They quickly disappeared into the back. A swing set took up most of the small, grass-covered area. A tree swing hung on a large oak that had probably been there thirty years.

"She's made a good life for her and Chloe." Sierra turned to Rafe. "We have to find them."

A slim figure moved across the kitchen window. Rafe tugged Sierra behind a large cypress, hunkering down beside her. He pulled a Glock from the back of his jeans. "Someone's inside."

Sierra gripped the bark and shifted her weight off her injured thigh. "A cop?"

"No police cars out front. I doubt it," Rafe said, with a suspicious glance at her leg. "How bad?" he asked.

"Fine."

Beads of sweat clung to her upper lip. She hurt. She couldn't hide the truth. "Stay put. I'll check it out. It could be your friend coming back to get the cat."

"It's not her," Sierra countered, slipping the gun from her bag.

"Just sit tight. Don't take any risks."

"I won't let them get away."

She'd tackle the guy if she had to. Which made it all the more important for Rafe to take care of this without getting Sierra involved.

He worked his way to the back door of the ranch-style house, each movement calculated to be silent, and sidled up to the door, his body taut, his face intense.

Behind the curtains a figure appeared. The silhouette shifted.

"Gun!" Sierra shouted from behind him.

Rafe cursed and burst through the door.

Chapter Four

Sierra raced from behind the cypress, limping as fast as her injured leg would allow. She ignored the pain radiating from her wound. Rafe had disappeared into Mallory's house without backup.

"Rafe?" she shouted.

A loud crash exploded from inside.

She stepped up on the rear porch. "I'm coming in!"

Before she could throw open the door, a figure slammed into her, knocking her onto her backside. He leaped over her and took off at a full sprint. She sat up and aimed her weapon, but she could barely make out his shadow in the moonlit night. "Stop!"

He didn't so much as pause, streaking away from her. Sierra hesitated, and he darted out of her line of sight toward the front of the house.

She vaulted to her feet to chase after him, but her leg buckled and her knees hit hard, crashing into the grass.

Rafe barreled out of the house. He skidded to a halt beside her. A scowl darkened his expression.

She waved him off. "I'm fine. Get him."

Rafe cast a quick glance at her with that this-isn't-over look. He'd just rounded the house's corner when tires squealed away.

Sierra lay on her back, gazing at the star-filled sky, trying to recall the man's features, but it had happened so fast.

Leather boots plodded over. Rafe knelt beside her. "You okay?"

"I didn't get a good look at his face," Sierra said, frowning, "but Bud is a lot stockier than that guy."

"Whoever he is, he wore a mask and boots and took off in that beat-up van. License plate was splattered in mud and unreadable." Rafe held out his hand and helped her to her feet, keeping hold of her shoulders to steady her. "Why the hell didn't you follow orders?"

"You can't be in two places at once." She tested the weight on her leg. Not bad, just not normal. "I'm fine," she repeated.

He glanced down at her thigh, then shoved

his hand through his hair. Not saying a word, he grunted and strode back into the house.

Sierra followed behind him and gasped when she entered her best friend's kitchen. Every cabinet had been opened, dishes broken. The place had been completely ransacked.

"I wonder how much of this the cops did when they searched the place," Sierra said, picking up a broken serving dish from the floor and setting it in the sink. "And how much that guy did."

"Hard to tell, but her ex is a bit lower on my list right now." Rafe crossed the kitchen and looked into the living room. "This room isn't much better. You said she'd taken files from work?"

Sierra stepped through the chaos. The sofa lay on its back. Photos that had decorated the entertainment center were knocked over. "I was working on the file before we left to pick up Chloe from school. I should've taken them with us." Sierra shook her head in disgust. "I left them on the coffee table."

"The cops found them. Since your friend wasn't supposed to have those records, it looks even worse."

He could've said so much more, but he didn't. She'd screwed up, and she knew it. She stared up at Rafe. "How do we find Mallory and Chloe?"

"You're the forensic accountant," Rafe said. "Go back to the beginning and follow the money."

"I need access to the rodeo's accounts." Sierra bit her lip. "I have an idea. It's a long shot, though."

She trudged up the stairs and entered Mallory's bedroom. The mattress had been up-ended, the drawers emptied. Rafe followed her, and she walked into the closet. More chaos, but Sierra shoved back some hangers. "When we were in college, Mallory had a jerk boyfriend who'd log on to her computer and buy stuff. She started hiding her passwords. She used it for personal stuff, but maybe—"

Sierra sank to the floor, ignoring the twinge in her leg. She tugged at the edge of the carpet in the corner of the closet and slipped out several sheets of paper.

Rafe knelt beside her. "The cops never would have found this. Neither would our burglar."

She unfolded one of the papers and scanned the document. "Account names and passwords for her personal bank account."

"Could come in handy," Rafe said.

With a glare, she snatched the paper back. He shrugged. "Just saying. We don't know what's really going on."

Her gaze narrowed at the second paper.

"These are the passwords for the rodeo." Sierra's gut sank when she read one entry. "Her boss's log in information is here, too."

"I see."

Rafe's tone gave away his skepticism.

"Lots of admins and accountants keep their boss's log-in info," she said.

"At home?"

She hated those short clipped sentences coming out of his mouth, but he had a point. Whatever her standard operating procedure at work, Mallory should *never* have kept her boss's logins at home. It simply didn't look good.

More than that, it looked downright bad. What had Mallory been thinking? Or doing?

Don't let your mind go there, Sierra. Her friend wasn't like that, and Sierra hated that she'd even let the possibility Mallory could be involved cross her mind. It seemed so disloyal, but Rafe's doubts had chipped away at her certainty.

What kind of friend did that make her?

Sierra didn't like that his distrust had poisoned her faith.

"You're wondering, aren't you?" he asked, his breath close to her ear.

Crouched in the corner of the closet, he leaned in closer, looking over her shoulder at the list, his heated body lightly touching her back. The light pine scent of his soap encircled her senses. She had no way to escape; he'd blocked her.

His presence melted into her. She resisted shifting closer, but her belly flip-flopped at the low baritone of his voice. Her brain screamed that she shouldn't be losing herself in the blind attraction she'd experienced the moment Noah had introduced them. She remembered it so well. She'd dreamed of those few seconds night after night, despite what he'd done.

His chocolate-brown gaze had swept over her body; his full lips had curved into a half smile. When he'd shaken her hand, his thumb had ever so slightly rubbed her palm. Sierra couldn't stop the shiver at the memory. Whatever he might be, Rafe Vargas defined sexy.

She cleared her throat.

He held out his hand and helped her to her feet. His dark eyes blazed. The room closed in around them. She couldn't look away. No doubt about it, Rafe was the kind of man you fantasized about, but not the kind you fell in love with. Not if you didn't want your heart broken and stomped on.

Despite the logic she swayed closer, seduced by the unvarnished passion in him. No wonder her body didn't listen to her mind.

Rafe's head lowered, just a bit. Slowly, seductively, temptingly. Her tongue licked her lips, wetting them. A deep growl rumbled from Rafe's chest.

A loud screech erupted from behind them. Rafe whirled around, weapon drawn. A ball of fur flew at him. He shouted and fell back into a slew of hangers and clothes.

Sierra stared down at the mostly white animal clinging to him.

Rafe lay on the floor glaring at the feline still digging its claws into his chest. "Princess Buttercup, I presume?"

THE SPOTLIGHT OF the moon and a few pinpricks of stars were the only light breaking through the cloak of darkness in front of the trailer.

Mallory's captor squeezed her arm and dragged her toward a rusted tin shed. She shifted her weight against him in resistance.

"Don't bother." He dug his fingers into her arm until she cried out. "Get inside."

The man shoved her through the door of the small building. She fell to her knees in the dark. Before she could stand, he strode in behind her and shut the door.

On all fours, Mallory's throat closed in panic. She squinted through blackness, but she couldn't see anything around her. The man hit a switch and a dim lightbulb hanging from an exposed wire crackled to life. Her gaze darted around the room. A chair sat in the center, a coil of rope huddled like a rattler lying in wait. A bat, its end stained with dark splotches, had been tossed nearby. Streaks of red and rust splattered the walls, a color that made her stomach churn.

Whatever he did, whatever happened, she had to survive. She had to get Chloe away from this place.

"Get up," he said, his voice soft and menacing. "And sit in the chair. We're going to have a little chat."

She hesitated.

"You do not want to challenge me. Not when I can destroy your world with a single order."

She swallowed with an audible gulp.

"That's right. Your daughter. I won't ask twice. In the chair. Now."

Legs shaking, she had no choice but to comply.

"Where are the files?" he asked.

She blinked. "At…at my house."

"Not those. We *have* those. I'm talking about the electronic files you copied."

Her eyes widened.

"Yes, we know. You made a big mistake, Mrs. Harrigan. Let's hope your daughter doesn't pay for your bad judgment."

Mallory could feel the blood drain from her cheeks. Her head spun. Oh God, he knew. She'd thought she'd covered her tracks so well. "I… I don't know—" she lied.

He bent over her and, with two fingers on either side of her windpipe, clutched her throat, squeezing hard. The world turned gray. Stars danced in front of her gaze. Blood roared through her head.

"Don't lie to me. The records weren't on your laptop or any of the equipment at your house. So where did you hide them?"

She grabbed at his hands, trying to pry his vise-like grip. She couldn't breathe. She blinked. She'd copied some files, but she hadn't had time to review them. She'd planned to give the thumb drive to Sierra. Now, it was hidden away in place she doubted anyone would find it. Even her best friend. Would this man make a deal? To save Chloe. And maybe even herself.

"Pl…please," she choked out. "I'll tell you."

He released her and shoved her away. The chair flew backward and clattered to the floor. Mallory's skull slammed against the dirt. She lay there for a moment, stunned.

"Pick up the chair and let's try this again." His large figure loomed over her, badge gleaming in the dim light.

Head throbbing and arms shaking, Mallory

struggled to her hands and knees, and rose. She righted the chair, hesitating, eyeing the distance between her and the door.

"Sit. Down."

She had no choice.

He crossed his arms, expression grim, unyielding. "Talk."

Mallory shivered under his gaze. She closed her eyes to work up her courage, finally opening them and staring him down, unblinking. For Chloe. "Let my daughter go, first."

The man's smile widened, his eyes wrinkling with satisfaction. "You think you can bargain with me? We'll see." He walked to the door. "Glen, bring the kid!" he shouted into the night.

What had she done? Mallory's entire body trembled. She'd made the wrong choice. *Please, God, don't let Chloe pay for my mistakes.*

Mallory squirmed in her seat under his stare and an enigmatic smile that caused a shiver to settle like a cold lump in her gut. After what seemed like forever, a soft knock tapped against the door. Glen's skin appeared almost green in the pale light of the shed. "Boss, are you sure—"

"Where's my mommy?" Chloe asked, her innocent voice piercing the tension. Mallory's chest tightened in fear.

Please let me do the right thing, say the right thing.

The cop threw open the door and grabbed Chloe like a sack of flour, holding her under his arm. The little girl screamed, kicking her feet.

"Shut up, kid."

Chloe went silent, and Mallory tried to smile at her daughter. She placed her finger to her lips and closed her eyes. Chloe nodded and squeezed her eyes tight, pressing her lips together. It was a game they'd played when Bud had gotten so drunk he'd been completely unpredictable.

"Get the hell out." The cop glared at Glen. "Think about what you have at stake. You know what we can do to you. And your family."

The cowboy's face went milk pale, and Glen gave the cop a quick nod. With a pitying glance at Mallory, he backed away, closing the door quietly, leaving them alone with a man who'd clearly left his oath by the wayside long ago.

The cop sat Chloe down, a harsh grip on her shoulders. "That's a good girl. Stay right there, where I can see you."

Eyes still closed, Chloe stumbled over the rope and fell to the ground. She sniffled, but didn't cry out.

"You trained her well," he said to Mallory. "Where are the files, and how many copies did you make? Tell me that, and I might let your kid leave here in one piece."

He slipped a knife from a scabbard and rested it against Mallory's neck. He nicked her throat.

Mallory froze. Chloe whimpered.

"Where?" he shouted and slapped her across the face. Mallory fell to her knees.

"No!" Chloe shouted. "You can't hurt Mommy!"

Chloe grabbed the baseball bat and swung with all her strength at the cop's legs, just like T-ball. The man's leg buckled, and he lunged at Chloe. Mallory twisted and yanked the bat from her daughter. She swung at his head. He fell to the floor.

Tears streaming down her face, Mallory grabbed Chloe into her arms and ran out of the shed. She raced toward the SUV and yanked open the door. No keys.

She spun back toward the yard. What now? Maybe the cop had them? A kickup of dust blurred the road. She recognized the shield on the side of the car. Cops. No time to search the man she might've killed.

At that moment, Glen opened the trailer door. He stared at them, eyes wide with shock. "You can't run," he yelled.

The hell they couldn't.

"Mommy?" Chloe whimpered.

Clutching her daughter, Mallory took off toward a grove of trees. She had to get as far away from the trailer as she could.

She looked back. Glen stood staring in disbelief.

Legs pumping, she raced across the field, nearly tripping more than once. Just as she reached the trees, shouts of fury slammed into her from behind. Three men were headed her way. Glen lay on the ground, still and unmoving.

Hugging Chloe tight, she peered into the wooded area. A path veered to the right. Mallory took off running to the left.

A branch slapped her face, cutting her. She blinked back the blood. No time to rest. She had to find help. She had no doubt if the cop caught up to her, she and Chloe were both dead.

UNDER THE COVER of night, Rafe escorted Sierra from Mallory's house to the truck. He placed her luggage and computer case behind the seat while she climbed into the passenger side.

He slammed the truck door and started the vehicle. Beside him, Sierra sat with the cat in her lap. The damned thing purred in ecstasy with each stroke of Sierra's hand. Rafe glared at the animal, but he couldn't stop himself from envying the beast's location. He wouldn't have minded lying in Sierra's lap being stroked. Hell, he might purr, too.

They hadn't found any other evidence pointing to Mallory and her daughter's whereabouts. With every hour, the chances of finding them both safe and alive diminished.

He recognized the tightness around Sierra's mouth, the worry creasing her forehead. There was nothing he could say that she didn't know. She might not do fieldwork, but she knew the statistics.

Her face was pale. The ibuprofen had to be wearing off, so he knew she was in pain. On a normal op he'd have headed straight to the rodeo—or called up Zane or Sierra to have them hack in.

He tapped his cell phone.

"Westin." Zane's voice carried over the phone. "I hope you found our missing chickadee, Rafe. Boss man isn't a happy camper, and that means the rest of us aren't, either."

Sierra frowned. "I'm right here, Zane."

"Oops. Hi, gorgeous. You sure know how to cause chaos."

"Like you don't," she retorted.

"Could you two give it a rest?" Rafe sighed. "Zane, we need you to hack into the San Antonio Rodeo. We're looking for—"

"They're moving money around. Fifty thousand at least," Sierra offered. "Can you identify who and how much? The evidence points to Mallory Harrigan, but she's being framed."

"That's one theory," Rafe interjected.

Zane was quiet for a moment. "I've followed that trail, Sierra. You sure it's a frame, because it doesn't look like it. There are deposits into a separate account under her name. She has access, and records show *she* transferred the money."

Sierra sighed. "You don't believe me, either."

Rafe grabbed the phone. "Mallory Harrigan's house was tossed. There's a kid in the mix. It's too easy, Zane."

She stared openmouthed at him. Was she that shocked at his defense of Mallory? He might have been skeptical of Sierra's best friend, but he couldn't deny the truth. Being agile—in body and mind—had kept him alive.

"I can see the bank accounts," Zane said, "but I haven't been able to access their books or their local system."

"Firewall?" Rafe scratched his temple.

Zane snorted and Sierra chuckled.

"What's so funny?" Rafe asked.

"A firewall wouldn't stop Zane," she said. "Or me. Are you thinking it's a stand-alone box?"

"We'd do better with a hands-on look," Zane added.

"Then we're going to the rodeo." Rafe glanced

at his watch. "If we don't check out that office tonight, we'll lose another dozen hours. It'll be too complicated to break in during daylight. Especially during the rodeo events."

"I'll keep working the search at this end," Zane said. "Let me know what I can do."

Rafe tapped his phone and glanced at Sierra searching for signs of pain or fatigue. Except for the faint tightness in her lips, she hid the pain well. "You up for a little nighttime surveillance?"

"If it gets us closer to finding Mallory and Chloe, do you even have to ask?"

With a quick twist in his seat, Rafe reached into his duffel and pulled out a bottle. "Take a couple more of these. You should be resting that leg."

Sierra downed the pills. "Thanks. Again."

It took about twenty minutes to reach the San Antonio Arena. The lot wasn't completely dark despite the late hour, with the minimum security lights bathing the asphalt in an eerie yellow glow.

He parked in a darkened corner and studied the layout. Leaving the truck close to the entrance might provide a quick entry, but it would attract attention.

Rafe opened the door, leaving the dang cat comfortably in the front seat. The creature circled and settled on the soft cushion, blinking her strange iridescent eyes.

With that pitiful expression, he couldn't *not* scratch Princess Buttercup's...okay, he had to stop with that name. He needed something not quite so...princess-y.

Perhaps P.B. for short. Not bad.

"I need to get to that rodeo office before they erase all traces of what happened," Sierra said, exiting the passenger side.

Rafe rounded the truck. "They know you escaped, and they know Mallory had access to the information. If she's innocent, chances are they've cleaned out the office of anything that doesn't support her guilt. The data is probably gone."

"There's a chance. Mallory could have hidden the records," Sierra said. "There are ways to recover erased files, unless they're using some very sophisticated file-wiping technology."

Rafe closed the door and locked it. "Let's get this over with. I don't like being out in the open with you on a bum leg."

She touched his arm. "Thank you, Rafe. For giving Mallory the benefit of the doubt."

"Don't thank me yet. Besides, I'm still not completely convinced your friend didn't betray you in the end. This doesn't smell right, but—"

Sierra dropped her hand. "Do you suspect everyone you meet?"

"Yes. Human beings are flawed. And no matter how good the intentions, most take the easy path."

Hadn't he done the same thing as a kid? Hadn't his brother? He never would've changed if his brother hadn't paid the ultimate price for his mistakes.

"You're wrong," she said with a sympathetic shake of her head. "Sometimes people are exactly who they appear to be."

"Like you?" Rafe quirked an eyebrow at her.

She met his gaze with a daggerlike glare.

"Just saying. You spent nearly a year hiding that you worked for CTC. You didn't come clean because it would cause conflict with your brothers and father. Easy route."

"You don't know anything about the situation," she said. "There was nothing easy about keeping the truth from my family. Don't judge what you can't understand."

Rafe shifted closer to her and tilted her chin up to his. "I know a hell of a lot about you, Sierra Bradford. More than you think." He dragged his finger down her cheek to her neck and along her collarbone.

She shivered at his touch. He should stop; he shouldn't tempt himself, or her, but he couldn't help it. Being this close to her made him want something real. And Sierra Bradford was the real deal, even with her secrets. Maybe because of them.

He lifted his other hand to her horribly bruised cheek. "I know a few spots that turn you on at the slightest touch." He leaned in closer and nipped her ear. The hairs on her arms stood up.

"I know you're as smart as Noah, even if you don't believe that." His lips inched along her jaw. "And I know you want more than anything to prove yourself, when you don't have to."

In one desperate motion his lips covered hers, gently. She groaned and opened herself to him. The flash of lightning he'd experienced the night they were together roared back. He tasted the sweetness of her lips and knew his body and his heart owned him at this moment. His head had gone AWOL.

Sierra clutched his shirt in her hands. Rafe wrapped his arms around her and pressed her against him, but when she let out a gasp of pain, he immediately released her. "God, I'm sorry."

She pulled back, her lips swollen, her gaze foggy. She blinked away the passion, her look one of caution. "I can't seem to resist you," she said softly.

"You'd tempt a saint," Rafe said. "And I've broken too many commandments to qualify."

She bit her lip. "You hurt me when you left that morning. How can I trust you?"

"You can't."

Chapter Five

The air grew heavy with humiliation. Sierra pulled away from Rafe. "You're honest at least."

Her body thrummed with unfulfilled need, but Sierra tamped it down. Rafe had the same idea. He shifted, and her gaze fell to the front of his jeans. He couldn't hide his wants. Then again, neither could she. Her nipples had gone hard, hypersensitive against the soft T-shirt she wore.

"Let's go inside," she said softly. "The sooner we find Mallory, the sooner you can go back to wherever you live and I can return to Denver."

And not have to see you.

She left the words unspoken, but they settled between them like a concrete wall dividing them.

As they made their way toward a side door at the arena, Rafe pulled out his phone and pressed a key.

Sierra leaned toward him taking a quick look at the app. "A jammer?"

"Your brother and Zane developed it. Just in case there are cameras. We don't need anyone tying us to this place."

Forty more yards and they reached the door. Rafe tested it. Locked.

He didn't hesitate, but reached into his pocket and pulled out two picks.

Within seconds the door opened and they entered the large space, the scent of livestock and hay floating on the air. Long, broad hallways led to the eerily silent arena, but they bypassed them and headed toward the row of offices.

"I expected to see crime scene tape," Sierra said.

"Could be enough political clout buys more than just a fixed parking ticket."

Sierra rubbed her nape, the tension coiling her muscles into stiff ropes. "We *have* to find a lead here. If we don't..."

"This isn't your fault."

"If I'd taken Mallory's concerns more seriously, recognized the danger, maybe I could've protected her." The guilt clawed at Sierra's throat. She'd relived every second of the sight of Mallory's resigned look when Chloe had frozen. Both women had known the chances of survival when that van had disappeared.

Rafe turned her into his arms. "Look at me."

She met his gaze, his brown eyes dark and intent.

"I've been in a lot of ops. More than my share have gone to hell. You can't look back, you have to look forward. After it's over you can regret and rehash all you want. Until the next op. If you don't, you'll make a mistake. You understand?"

Sierra nodded. "Focus on the here and now. I can do that." Maybe.

The freight elevator rumbled to her right. Rafe shoved her behind a pillar and pressed her tight against the concrete. She held her breath.

Footsteps strode past them. Rafe eased them around the column to keep out of the guard's sight. Finally the echo of the boots faded away.

She let out a long, slow breath.

"Let's move," he whispered. "As quietly as you can."

Without a sound they hurried to the office door. Rafe made quick work of the lock. He opened it and snuck through before shutting it behind them. He tugged the shade down, blocking the door's glass window to outside light. The room went dark.

Sierra dug into her side pocket for the small but powerful flashlight Noah had given her to carry on her key ring. She doubted he'd expected her to use it for breaking and entering.

"Nice. You're a regular Girl Scout. Keep the light pointed down so you don't attract attention," Rafe said. "Which computer?"

"There." She nodded at Mallory's nameplate on a desk facing the entrance. "I'm surprised they haven't confiscated it."

"It shouldn't be there." Rafe scowled. "This was too easy. Gives me a bad feeling."

"Maybe our luck is changing." Sierra rounded the desk. Give her a keyboard and a mouse, and she could do anything.

Rafe planted himself near the door. She fired up the machine, biting her lip at the light glowing from the monitor. At least it was facing away from the entrance. Still, she dimmed the screen. Hopefully no one would notice.

Holding the flashlight in her mouth, Sierra searched the desk and tugged a ledger from the drawer. She pulled out a receipt file and walked through the bank statements. She had to figure out why the numbers didn't match up.

With every line, her frown deepened. The longer she tracked, the more the back of her neck prickled. Sierra knew Mallory's capabilities. They'd gone to school together. Attended the same classes. There were too many mistakes. Nothing too large, but added up, over one million dollars so far.

Any first year accounting student could find the errors in these books by simply matching cash transactions with no pedigree. What was she missing? Or had Mallory left the trail on purpose?

Rafe cleared his throat and pointed at his watch. She nodded.

She snapped photos of the documents before pushing aside the ledger. With a click of the mouse, she opened the bank records directory on the computer. Something wasn't quite right. She studied the directory. Bigger than she'd expected. The individual files didn't jibe with the folder size. She quickly pulled up the command prompt window and typed in a few keystrokes. The view changed. Voilà. An invisible file. A *locked* invisible file.

Interesting.

She clicked on it. Password protected. Which wasn't a problem. Most people used simple passwords easily deciphered. Or, in Sierra's case, easily circumvented.

Her decryption tool did its work within minutes and she opened the file. She scanned a few rows. Right there, on the spreadsheet. The truth. Maybe not who or why, but how much.

Sierra quickly calculated the total in her head. She let out a low whistle.

Rafe's head snapped up and he walked to her, leaning over. His warm hand squeezed her shoulder. "What've you found?"

"Whoever kept this second set of books has laundered nearly five million dollars in the last year alone," she whispered.

"That's willing-to-kill money," he said with a frown.

Sierra met Rafe's gaze. "If Mallory discovered this file—"

"She's in bigger trouble than we thought."

"The records go back at least five years." Sierra rubbed her eyes as if refocusing them would change the facts. It didn't, of course. "If the previous years' were comparable to this last one, that's twenty-five million."

"We're talking a significant amount of money. With that much on the line, people get desperate. And deadly."

Rafe straightened, his frown deepening. The concern in his eyes sent a skitter of worry snaking up and down Sierra's back.

"You don't think they're—"

She couldn't say the word aloud. Rafe knelt in front of the chair and clasped her hands in his, meeting her gaze, his face half-covered in shadow in the dim light. "If all they'd wanted was to silence her, they could have killed her on the side of the road. They needed her. For something. There's a chance."

But not a good one. She recognized the truth in his expression.

"Give me a name, Sierra," Rafe whispered. "And I'll do whatever it takes to get them back."

"I'll find something," she promised, as much to herself as to him, hoping to God she spoke the truth. If they kept records of transactions, maybe, just maybe she'd uncover some identifying information. With a prayer on her lips, she selected another work sheet and scanned the text.

"You shouldn't be here," a male voice hissed from outside the door, only a few feet away.

Sierra's hand froze, tightening on the mouse. Oh God. Her gaze snapped to Rafe. His expression had gone cold and lethal. He rose, his movements silent, and pressed his finger to his lips.

With the precision of a jungle cat, he padded to the door without making a sound and slipped his weapon from its holster.

"We have to talk," another voice, urgent, almost desperate, whispered. "It can't wait."

Her heart thudded in her chest. How many people would be hovering right outside this particular office door? What if the two men came into the office? She swallowed hard. Her hands shook. She was so close to finding an answer.

Any moment now, the chance could be gone. She had to be quick. They needed this information. Hands shaking, she pulled out a thumb drive and quickly saved the file. Within seconds she'd closed down the computer system, leaving everything as she'd found it.

"We can't be seen together," the first man snapped. He jiggled the doorknob. "Damn. Where's that key?"

Their luck had run out. Rafe nodded toward her right. Her gaze followed his line of sight. Just a few feet from her a door was propped open. To a closet.

A small, tight space. Too much like another closet. The one where Sierra had almost died, where Archimedes had carved his symbol into her skin, leaving his mark forever. Her heart raced. A familiar vise closed off her breathing at the thought of entering the tiny room. No way could she go in there. She shook her head and pulled out her weapon.

He tapped his ear. She understood the signal. Rafe *could* take the men by surprise, but he didn't want to interrupt their conversation. Their chance to save Mallory depended on finding her quickly. They needed the intel first.

Rafe's jaw muscles pulsed. He pointed underneath the desk. Okay, it might be tight, but she could manage to fold her five-foot-ten-inch frame under the furniture to hide. If she had to.

"This is urgent," the second man said.

Sierra eased the chair back. A small squeak sounded from the wheels. She froze.

"Fine. But be quick. The guard's round takes about a half hour." The gravelly voice didn't sound familiar to her, except for the West Texas twang. "What's so damned important you had to pull me away from a good steak?"

"I'm getting pressure from one of our buyers. They want proof we have the real thing."

The first man let out a snort. "Cut 'em loose. We have other opportunities."

"Umm… It's not that easy. They've threatened to go to the cops."

A harsh curse echoed through the door.

"You came to me with this idea to expand our base, and I gave you one damned job. Vet the customers. I've been running this operation out of the rodeo for over five years, and no one has *ever* threatened me with the cops. Until you screwed it up."

"They're a high bidder." The man's voice trembled. "Double what you made on any one transaction last year."

"Really? That much?" The smoke-laced tone

turned speculative. "Show them the stuff. Keep them happy."

"They could still talk."

"High bidder. They want it bad. They were willing to talk to you. That means they're willing to walk outside the law. They're bluffing. They won't turn us in. Now get out of here. And don't be seen."

One set of footsteps hurried away. The other man gave a huff. "Amateur," he muttered.

Not a word about Mallory, but she and Rafe needed an identity. They couldn't let him get away.

She rose from her hiding place and pulled out her weapon. Rafe must've been thinking the same thing. He placed his hand on the doorknob and gave her a questioning look. She nodded.

"Sir, what are you doing here? This is a closed area." A questioning voice intruded.

A gunshot rang out, followed by a loud curse. Rafe flung open the door. Sierra sprang from her position to follow. The guard lay in a pool of blood. A figure disappeared to the front of the arena.

Rafe gripped his weapon. "I'll—"

"Help me," the injured guard whispered through gurgling breath. "Please."

Tires squealed. The guy must've had a waiting vehicle. And since they'd jammed the cameras, there'd be no video to identify it.

Rafe knelt beside the man. He opened his shirt. Buttons flew everywhere, and Rafe let out a curse. "I need another set of hands," he said, tugging off his own shirt and pressing it to the bloody wound. "Put pressure on the wound."

She held the material down.

He flattened his hands over hers. "Harder. We have to stop the bleeding."

Sierra rose to her knees to get better leverage. "I've got it."

Rafe removed his hands and nodded. He wiped one hand on his shirt and palmed his phone. "Keep at it while I call for an ambulance. I don't want your voice on record. As it is, this is going to take a lot of tap-dancing."

Dawn was Rafe's enemy. It would arrive soon, and the sky had lightened too much for his liking. Light meant clarity, and he preferred to move in the murk. Less likely to be identified.

He peered around the end trailer where he'd been observing the chaos at the arena. The ambulance screamed away from the arena. Hopefully the guard would survive.

The crime scene unit had arrived. Crime scene tape littered the area. Numerous uniforms milled about the scene. On another mission, he might have recruited them to help with their search. More manpower could mean finding Mallory Harrigan and her little girl faster—or discovering a weak link in the organization— but not this operation. He was convinced the chances of Sierra's friend and her daughter surviving depended on secrecy. They were on their own except for a few trusted allies.

His gaze shifted to a side road out of the line of sight of the arena. Sierra waited there. Once he'd made the emergency call, he'd sent her back to the truck partly to work on the files, but mainly to protect her. He had no idea if one of the cops had been on the road that night when Mallory and Chloe had been abducted, and he wasn't taking any chances. She was safe in his truck a good half mile away with a thumb drive that he hoped gave them a name, because whoever shot the security guard hadn't revealed enough information to be of any use. Rafe would recognize the boss's voice if he heard it again, though. He also had his theories. Given the talk of buyers and sellers this close to the border, they were pretty much referencing guns or drugs. Which could mean cartels. What a cluster.

Rafe studied an older man, a bit stocky, with a close haircut, wearing a Stetson, as he paced back and forth. He'd arrived in a Texas-sized Cadillac. A gold ring gleamed on his right hand. "And what the hell am I supposed to do about this?" he shouted, his voice carrying easily to Rafe. "I got a rodeo to run. You get your men to work faster, Captain. Or I'll make a phone call you won't appreciate."

A captain didn't typically work a scene in the middle of the night. Obviously the gentleman had clout. Which put him on the top of Rafe's suspect list.

A familiar detective standing at the perimeter eased away from the group, and after a quick backward glance, strode toward Rafe. The man was skilled and subtle at blending into the scenery, Rafe would give him that.

Detective Cade Foster rounded the trailer where Rafe had planted himself to observe. "Ransom is damned lucky I live fifteen minutes from this place. Another five and you'd be sitting in jail."

"Noted," Rafe said. "How's the guard?"

"Probably gonna make it. Thanks to you. Which is the reason I'm giving you the benefit of the doubt. That and I owe Ransom." Cade tilted his Stetson back, his frown deepening. "You're involved with the embezzlement case that hit yesterday? Mallory Harrigan. She shoot the guy?"

Rafe shook his head. "Pretty sure the perp was a man. I didn't get a good enough look to identify him, but he was around six feet, stocky, wore a white Stetson, a Western-style black suit and too-shiny cowboy boots. He drove off in a dark F350."

Cade flipped open a notebook and penned a few words. "Pretty specific, but not unlike a hundred thousand other men in this part of Texas."

"I know." Rafe scowled. "We're on a time crunch. You hear anything—"

"If it's pertinent, I'll contact you or Ransom. But quid pro quo. I want to be kept in the loop, or I come looking for you."

With a quick nod of agreement, Rafe shook Cade's hand. "We owe you."

"And I'll be collecting."

The detective headed back to the crime scene, and Rafe walked as quickly as he dared, not to attract attention. Early-morning shadows offered some cover, but that would end soon.

His phone vibrated, and he winced when he saw the screen identifying his boss.

"Vargas."

"What the hell is going on down there, Rafe?" Ransom didn't mince words. "Attempted murder, bringing in local law enforcement. You got me playing in the dark gray, and I don't like working there. Not on this side of the pond."

Rafe sighed. He'd thought about his choices, and they were few. And they involved CTC. "Sierra's stumbled onto something bigger than we thought." Rafe briefed his boss and winced at the man's curses.

"You believe the woman and girl are alive?" Ransom asked.

"*If* she can hold out and not give them what they want, maybe." Truth was, after the way the guard had been shot, Rafe was less certain than he had been. The bad guys may just cut their losses. If they owned a wide enough swath of law-enforcement officials, they could probably squelch most evidence. He and Ransom had seen it happen more than once.

"The guy shot a security guard, risking scrutiny just to hide a conversation," Ransom said. "That's no coincidence."

"Agreed. Since Sierra found evidence of at least twenty-five million being laundered through the rodeo, and these guys are working a deal that could bring in twice that over five years, I'd say they have a lot to lose. Sierra's working the electrons, boss, but we don't have a name. Not even close. If we're going to save Mallory and Chloe, we need information. And even if Cade were willing to risk his career, I don't know who's involved at the San Antonio PD."

"What are you proposing?"

"If we're going to follow the money, Sierra and I need an in at the San Antonio Rodeo. Can you do it?" Actually, Rafe had no doubts Ransom could pull it off. The trouble was, did he want to?

"Identities for *both* of you? Can't you just send her home? She doesn't have the field experience for undercover."

"She's a lot like her brother once she has a mission in her head. She won't leave. Mallory and Chloe are important to her. Besides, I need her to follow the money."

Ransom let out a curse. "She's as much of a pain in the ass as Noah." The sound of drumming fingers filtered through the phone. "We might be able to switch you out for someone already entered in the rodeo. You did some bull riding when you were young, right?"

Like Ransom didn't know, or remember.

"It's been a while. I gave it up. Special Forces was less dangerous," Rafe said.

"With your pedigree, I think I know someone who can find you a spot. You *sure* Sierra won't let this alone?"

"No way. It's too personal. Which worries me, but the truth is, she knows the players better than I do. She may have heard something or seen something that will break the case. It's her best friend and five-year-old goddaughter. If it doesn't turn out well and we don't let her help…" He left the consequences unsaid. No need. Just the thought made Rafe's gut twist. "How do I argue with that?"

"Noah's going to kill us both when he learns she's gone undercover. Even if you're watching out for her." Ransom's voice sounded pained.

"He hasn't forgiven you yet, has he?" Rafe said. "For keeping Sierra's employment a secret for so long?"

"He flew down here just to slug me," Ransom admitted. "Guy has a killer left hook."

"Next time I'm in Carder, I might do the same."

"You both need to see Sierra for who she is. The best I've seen. That's why I hired her in the first place."

"At the computer," Rafe said, "I'd agree with you. But you took her off duty."

"For her. Not for you and Noah. She wanted to be more involved, to get hands-on experience. Archimedes's abduction gave her a look into what could happen. Made her skittish. She needed time to heal, to decide. From what Noah's said, she's not quite ready."

"I'm well aware. I'm keeping an eye on her."

"Anything happens to her, Noah and her other brothers won't let you forget it."

"If anything happens to her, it'll happen to me first," Rafe muttered. "I'll try to convince her to go home, but we both know the odds."

"Zero. Do you need backup for the op?"

"I need someone in that rodeo office with ready access to records and to run interference. I don't want Sierra put in that position. Three of these guys have seen her. Even with the disguise I have planned, I'm concerned."

"Zane's on his way since you've already read him in."

At the words, Rafe coughed.

Ransom let out a low chuckle. "You think I didn't know he was running a search for you? Really, Rafe? It takes a lot to surprise me." Ransom paused. "By the way, did you forget to mention a certain *package* you had delivered?"

Package? It took Rafe a moment. He hadn't called it in. He grimaced. "Elena. Yeah. I—"

"Another stray. I won't out you as a closet softy, Rafe. Besides, she deserves a break. The wife and kids have fallen in love with her and Charlie. I have a place for them. Give me a heads-up next time. Our security spooked her."

"She okay?"

"She's tough. And there's a bit more to her than you suspected, I think. I'll give you the details later. Back to our immediate problem. I'm using Zane as a go-between with Detective Foster until this op is over. Afterward, you, Noah and I are having a long conversation regarding Sierra."

Ransom ended the phone call, and Rafe picked up his pace heading to his truck. Was he making a mistake?

Normally, when the plan took shape, his entire body went calm and still. Not this morning. He vibrated with tension. Probably due to working with another woman he cared about. He couldn't deny his feelings for Sierra. And he couldn't stop the memories of the fallout of the last op with his fiancée. Her bullet-ridden body, the blood. Arriving too late.

He reached the vehicle and gripped the door handle with whitened knuckles. The bruises on Sierra's face had deepened in color. She sat hunched over the computer, lost in concentration.

He'd have to work on her spatial awareness. The angry bullet's graze on her thigh burned in his memory. She could've been killed, and everything inside Rafe shouted at him to pack her in Bubble Wrap and hide her away. Instead, he rapped on the window.

Sierra jerked her head up. Princess Buttercup leaped across the keyboard and placed her paws on the window.

The shock on Sierra's face melted into relief, and she rolled down the glass. "You're back. I was worried the cops…"

"Ransom's guy came through."

"Thank goodness." She let out a shuddering breath. "I half expected him to be on the take."

"We can trust Cade." He frowned. "But you can't let yourself get so immersed in your work that you're that easily surprised. I could have dropped you if I'd wanted to."

"I was tracking your movements," she said with a confident smile. "I saw your approach. I just didn't expect you to bang on the window. Don't do that again."

Rafe rubbed the brow bone over his uncovered eye. This op was going to test his patience in a big way.

The dang cat butted her head through the open window against Rafe's forearm. He shook his head but scratched the silly animal's ears anyway. "I'm not sure what Ransom did for the detective, but whatever it was, Cade was willing to risk lying to his superiors about finding the guard. He's covering for us. For now anyway."

"Is the guard going to make it?"

"He'll be out of it for a while, but it looks like it."

Sierra let out a sigh of relief.

"You get a name?" he asked.

"Nothing." Her brow furrowed, and her eyes flashed with fury. "Millions of dollars are moving through that rodeo. Whoever's doing this is smart, and secretive. We know the what, but the who and why are like smoke. No account numbers, no bank routing numbers, nothing to identify them. I've hit a brick wall."

Rafe leaned in. "Look, honey, this situation is getting complicated. And more dangerous. Following the ones and zeroes won't cut it. We need boots-on-the-ground intel if we're going to find Mallory and Chloe."

"The rodeo venue's owner is John Beckel. I'm running his background next."

"Good idea. See if anything pops." Rafe shifted his feet. "Sierra, why not head up to Carder? CTC headquarters has the latest equipment, everything you need to work your magic."

She froze and narrowed her gaze at him. "I need to be here. You need backup."

"Zane's coming in. I promise, I'll let you know what's happening every step of the way."

"You want to get rid of me. Why?" With a snap, she closed the laptop.

"You're good at your job. You can help us there."

"Mallory's told me about her job, about the rodeo. I can help more right here during the investigation…"

Her words tapered off, and her eyes widened. "You're going undercover. That's what you meant by boots on the ground."

He could almost see the gears churning in her mind. The eagerness in her eyes made his gut twist. He knew the adrenaline rush well, and he knew the risks. She had a personal investment in this op. It made for bad decision making. He should know.

She gripped his arm. "I can help you."

"If I said no, you'd insert yourself anyway, wouldn't you? Somehow, some way?"

"Let's put it this way. You aren't banishing me to Carder, anytime soon. Not until Mallory and Chloe are home safe and sound." She met his gaze. "I can't stop looking for them. Not when I should've been able to stop them from being taken."

He gripped the door through the open window. "Then I guess it's time for us to go undercover at the rodeo."

Chapter Six

A thin layer of pink-orange sky filtered through the trees. Hunkered in a depression in the midst of a small but thick grove of cottonwood trees, Mallory cradled Chloe, focusing on her daughter's even breathing. She'd finally fallen asleep. Even though Mallory could use the rest, she couldn't close her eyes. She peered through the web of branches encasing them, praying she saw nothing. That they were safe.

She'd had no idea how far they'd run, or how long. The only light visible had been a shard of moon hanging in the sky and a bevy of stars, which had offered little hope. She'd seen no sign of civilization anywhere. Not a road, not a light. Just darkness and trees and open stretches of land.

They'd almost been caught, but choosing the road less traveled had been their salvation. Finally, when the shouts and curses of their captors had dimmed, they'd trudged as long as Chloe's legs had held out. Mallory had carried her daughter as long as she could, until, finally, legs and arms shaking, she'd stumbled and pitched to the ground. She had no choice but to stop. Mallory had crawled underneath a mesh of leaves and branches. She'd camouflaged their hideout to the best of her ability and settled in for the remainder of the night.

Darkness had provided camouflage, but now that dawn had peeked over the horizon, it would be more difficult than ever to escape detection. She stroked Chloe's hair. Tears pricked the corners of Mallory's eyes.

Their escape had been so panicked, the desperation to survive so paramount, she hadn't kept track of which direction they'd run.

If she left their hideout, she could very well end up going back toward that trailer—and their kidnappers.

Chloe squirmed in her lap. "Mommy," she whimpered.

"Shh, Button. You have to be very, very quiet."

"Or the bad people will find us." The little girl burrowed against her mother's breast.

"Yes." Mallory kissed the top of her daughter's head.

"The sun's up. I'm hungry."

"I know, but we can't eat right now. Maybe a little later, okay?"

"Pancakes?"

If only she possessed Chloe's optimism. "Maybe tomorrow," she said, praying she told her daughter the truth.

"That means no," Chloe said, pouting. She squirmed. "Mommy, I have to go pottie."

"Okay, sugar, but we need to stay quiet."

Chloe pursed her lips and nodded. Carefully Mallory pushed aside the leaves, and they crawled out of their hiding place. Mallory stood and took her daughter over to a stand of buffalo grass near a small grove of trees.

A shout carried through the landscape. "Find them! Ten grand to whoever brings them to me. Dead or alive."

Mallory's throat spasmed in panic. She grabbed her daughter's hand. "Run, Chloe! Run!"

SIERRA RUBBED HER EYES. She winced at the grit and stinging behind her lids. She'd been through more than her share of all-nighters during college, but she was out of practice. The morning sun had only risen a sliver, and the western sky still bore that dark purple-blue of night.

Rafe pulled into the motel parking lot. Princess Buttercup had plastered herself to his leg. If he moved an inch, the cat scooted closer.

Covering her mouth with her hand to disguise her small smile, Sierra eyed the pair. He didn't quite know what to make of the mostly white calico, but he sure couldn't shake that cat.

After Rafe turned off the engine, he twisted in his seat, once again pushing Princess Buttercup out of the way, gently but firmly. The cat lightly jumped onto the floor and curled around Rafe's boots. He shook his head, clearly befuddled. "Are cats trainable? At all?"

She bit the inside of her cheek. "About as much as you are."

A twinkle of humor shined in his unpatched eye. She couldn't ever remember witnessing that particular expression on his face. She liked the change, but it didn't last long. He stroked his chin. "You want to be part of this op, I have some ground rules, or we end this here and now. First one is, this is my operation. I say jump, you ask how high. I give an order, you don't question me because I may not have time to explain myself. Got it?"

She bristled at the order but knew he was right. He had the experience; she was a newbie. "Got it."

In truth, she couldn't believe he'd agreed to work with her. She knew from the jobs Ransom assigned to Rafe that he didn't do partners. Not if he could help it. But, she possessed a skill he didn't. She might excel at her job as a forensic accountant, but she also knew Rafe. He was a lone wolf. He preferred swooping in, getting the job done as quickly as possible—on his own—and swooping out, not getting too involved. Her brother had tried to warn her off when she'd been under the illusion that there might be something between her and Rafe. The warning had come too late. She'd already fallen for that mysterious aura he exuded.

Everything about him should have terrified her—the edge of danger lacing his eyes, the intensity, the aloofness. Perhaps because she'd worn her own mask for far too long, she'd recognized something more beneath the mask he wore. A kindred spirit.

He was also a true hero at heart. Mallory and Chloe were innocent. And Rafe would do whatever it took to find them. Even if it meant teaming with a beginner.

"First order of business is to move locations. We clean out the motel room and disappear. No trace. Eliminate any possibility of a tail."

Nodding, she slid out of the truck. Her leg had gone stiff after sitting so long, but at least it didn't hurt quite as much. She could feel his narrowed gaze watching her, studying her movement. She stiffened, sucking up the pain so her walk appeared even and natural.

His frown deepened, but he didn't comment. They walked to the motel room.

"Key?" he asked, holding out his hand.

Ignoring him, she unlocked the door. When she pushed it open, she couldn't stop her gasp. The room had been destroyed.

Rafe shoved her away from the entrance with one hand and unholstered his weapon with the other. Sierra wasn't nearly as quick, but she drew the Glock.

He quickly searched the small bathroom and closet. "Clear."

Stepping across the threshold, she surveyed the destruction. The drawers had been pulled out, the mattress tossed, nothing left untouched, though truth be told, she hadn't had much.

"How did they find me?"

"The same way I did. Which means they have resources. Not surprising, but definitely problematic."

A knock sounded on the half-open door. "Did your brother find you, Mrs. Jones?" the hotel manager asked, barging in. His eyes went wide with shock, and he gasped. "What have you done? Who's going to pay for this?"

Rafe tugged a wad of cash from his pocket and thrust several hundred-dollar bills into the manager's hands. "That should cover it. We'll be out of here in five minutes," he said, shoving the man out the door.

He grumbled, giving them both a dirty look before he walked away.

"Go out to the car," Rafe said.

"What are you going to do?"

"Make certain our friends didn't leave any unexpected presents."

"How can I help?" she asked.

"Know anything about explosive devices?"

Her cheeks heated, and she backed out of the room. "Be careful, Rafe."

He shot her a grin. "Always."

"And never," she muttered.

Sierra couldn't just sit in the truck waiting for the room to explode. She paced back and forth, her hand wrapped around her weapon. Princess Buttercup peered out from inside the truck, her white face tilted, and the rust and black decorating her ears and top of her head looking like a crown.

"You know something's not right, too, don't you, baby?" Sierra said, making her way over to the truck door.

Rafe strode outside with a bag in his hand and tossed it into the Dumpster across the parking lot, veering toward the motel office.

A few minutes later he opened the truck

door. "The only description of your brother he gave me was a 'cowboy.' Narrows it down to half the city. At least they only tossed the place. We were lucky." He frowned at her. "They couldn't have taken any identifying information in the room?"

She shot him a heated glare.

"Then we're okay. For now." He paused and stared at the cat. "You think you could hold the beast while I drive. She's…distracting."

Sierra rounded the truck, opened the door and Princess Buttercup jumped into her arms. Sierra stroked her soft fur. "Sure thing."

But the moment Rafe joined her, the princess settled into her spot right next to him.

"I guess she likes you."

Rafe tossed his Stetson on the dash. "Now I know why I never had a pet."

He pulled onto the road and took off into the early-morning San Antonio traffic.

"Where are we going?"

"For now I'm making damn sure we aren't being tailed. After that…" He smiled at her.

She didn't like the look on his face.

Rafe shrugged. "We're getting married."

An hour of driving inanely around San Antonio had convinced Rafe no one was following them. Rush hour had begun, and the purr of the truck had lulled Sierra to sleep after she'd recovered from the shock of his *proposal*.

The shadows under her lashes made him frown. Was he making another huge mistake letting her be involved? He nearly laughed. Hell, he wasn't *allowing* her to do anything. Better that he work with her than have her as a loose cannon.

Still, anyone who would abduct a child would do anything.

He pulled in at an out-of-the-way motel with the truck facing so Sierra was protected from view.

"Watch out for her, P.B.," he muttered to the cat. The animal licked its paws and gave a soft meow.

Rafe scratched the beast's ears. A rumble-like purr vibrated in her chest. Stunned at the turn his life had taken—from black ops in Afghanistan to talking to a cat named Princess Buttercup in San Antonio—he strode into the motel's office.

The dated room appeared spotless. Before Rafe could sound the small bell on the reservation counter, a man with the look of an ex-boxer, his nose obviously broken more than once, appeared through a doorway to what appeared to be his apartment.

Within moments, Rafe had paid cash for a

couple of nights and signed in under a false name. The guy rang up the transaction without a word.

Rafe studied the man for a moment, then slid a couple hundred dollars across the counter. "I'm not expecting any visitors unless I introduce them to you personally. You got me?"

The guy didn't touch the money. A frown cut the line down the middle of his forehead into a crater. "I run an honest place. You up to any funny business, there's a better location half a block down the road."

Rafe's gaze centered on the guy's tattoo signifying Special Forces. "I just want quiet," Rafe said. "I think I can get that here."

The guy studied Rafe for a few seconds. "Marines or Rangers?" he asked.

"Green Beret. Four tours. You?"

"Two with the Rangers. I made it back, but my brother died in Afghanistan. Near Kandahar." The man slid Rafe's money back across the counter. "Name's Calhoun. Anyone asks, you ain't here and never have been. Just keep it on the up-and-up."

"You got it." Rafe took the key and strode out the door.

He scooted into the truck and drove to the end of the motel strip. Sierra didn't budge from her sound sleep. Rafe couldn't remember the last time he'd rested so…okay, maybe he could. In her arms a couple months ago.

Leaving her inside, he surveilled the motel room and unloaded the truck before opening the passenger door. He lifted her into his arms.

"You coming, P.B.?" he asked the cat. With a flick of her tail and a disdainful look down her feline nose, she bounded out of the vehicle and followed him inside.

Rafe shut the door closed with his foot, then laid Sierra on the bed, slipped off her shoes and tossed a spare blanket over her. He should clean her wound again, but he'd do that when she woke up.

He locked the door and closed the curtains. No one had seen them enter, so when a completely different couple exited, there would be no surprises. He tapped his phone.

"Westin. How's it going, Rafe?"

"We're in place. When do you get here?"

"A few hours. I've got your supplies. Jared King is coming with your horse and a hell of a tall tale for the owner of the rodeo. Should be there by this afternoon sometime."

"Good." After ending the call, he grabbed a couple of metal bowls, doled out water and cat food, then set up a litter box.

"I can't believe I'm doing this," he muttered.

Small, cute snores escaped Sierra. Rafe settled on the bed beside her. She turned toward him and nestled against his chest, wrapping her arm around him, then heaving a slow, contented sigh. Rafe stared at the ceiling above him. That morning almost two months ago flashed through him. A lifetime ago. A world ago. He'd never thought they'd share the same bed again.

P.B. pounced onto the mattress. She circled around and settled at his feet, purring softly.

He glanced at the woman lying next to him, and the cat with its head on his leg, hemming him in.

A throbbing headache pulsed behind Rafe's eyes. He shifted his patch. Until they found Mallory and Chloe, he was in big, big trouble, and there was absolutely no way to escape.

He was well and truly caught.

ONE SHARP KNOCK followed by two quick raps snapped Rafe from sleep. His left hand automatically reached for his weapon. His right hand was busy holding Sierra next to him. She wasn't lying on top of him like she had the last time they'd slept together, but she'd thrown one leg across his body. Gently he eased from beneath her. Princess Buttercup opened one eye, stared at him, then settled back down.

"Some watch cat you are," he muttered.

One glance through the peephole and he opened the door, closing it behind him to greet Zane.

Across the parking lot, Calhoun stared intently at them from the motel's office. Rafe gave the guy a brief nod, and he disappeared into the office.

"Special Forces?" Zane asked, crossing his burly arms across his body.

"Ranger." No one looked less like a geek than Zane with his football-player frame and tats down one arm. Personally, Rafe got the impression Zane enjoyed the disconnect.

"She inside?" Zane asked, not bothering to elaborate. They both knew who they were talking about.

Rafe nodded.

"She okay?"

"It's just a graze." Rafe glanced down at two large duffels. "Is that everything?"

Zane nodded. "Jared King's towing Ironsides and the rest of the equipment. You going to be able to pull this off?"

"We'll find out. It's been a decade since I've been in the arena."

Zane grinned. "I wasn't talking about the rodeo, Rafe. I meant Sierra. And Noah when he finds out you two have a less-than-legal marriage license."

"Under the names Rafe and Sarah Vargas. It's not real."

"You keep telling yourself that. You've got it as bad as Noah."

Rafe scowled at his friend. Zane just smiled. "Jared will be here in a couple of hours. You'll need that long to get ready. I'll see you at the rodeo."

Zane pulled out of the parking lot and Rafe carried the large duffels into the room.

"Who were you talking to?" Sierra sat up in bed and rubbed her eyes. Her light brown hair flowed over her shoulders.

"Zane. He delivered our disguises. The men who kidnapped Mallory and Chloe saw you, so we need a cover."

"You've come up with something. Obviously."

"It's best to keep the story as close to real as possible. I'm Rafe Vargas, former teen bull riding champ. I joined the military, was dishonorably discharged after getting caught smuggling and was released from prison last year. I've bought my way in with some high stakes that I don't talk about. And you, my dear, are my wife."

"I thought you were joking before. Married?" Sierra's face had gone pale.

"The rodeo's like a family. There's an entire subculture. Families, groupies, wives, girl-friends. Best way to find out where the money's flowing is to cover both sides."

"How do you know so much about it?"

"I rode when I was a kid. Before I enlisted when I turned eighteen."

He unzipped the bag and showed her the marriage license.

"Sarah?" she asked, staring at the paper. She let the marriage license flutter to the bed and studied him with a quizzical look on her face. "How much of what you just told me is true?"

"Like I said. It's easier to stay as close to the truth as possible." Rafe shrugged. How was he supposed to explain that last mission, Gabriella's death, his fight for freedom, and the justice he'd exacted on the men who'd betrayed them? What was the point? Instead of answering, he bent over the duffel.

"You'll need to blend in, and not stand out." Rafe tossed an auburn wig at her, a hairnet and some clothes. Finally he pulled out a bra attached to a large silicon mound.

Sierra poked at the fake belly. "I'm pregnant?"

"My other choice was a hot girlfriend. You'd attract too much attention." He frowned as the neck of his T-shirt slipped down her right shoulder, revealing soft skin and the upper curve of her breast.

Her cheeks reddened, and she readjusted her top.

He cleared his throat. "No single guy should give a pregnant woman a second look. Most will probably avoid looking at you."

"And you think this will work?"

"The men trying to find you won't be looking for a redhead who's five months pregnant."

She picked up the device and weighed it in her hand. "I've never done anything like this before, Rafe. I don't know how to act pregnant, or pump people for information."

"You're smart and resourceful. You know what we need to find out, you know what Mallory said and what her skills are, and you know better than anyone else how people hide money. You can do this." He tilted her face so her gaze met his. "Would I rather you were home in Denver safe and sound? Absolutely. But not because you can't do this job."

She fingered the clothes. "I've always worked behind the scenes. I thought you'd put me in that office to work the computer."

"Zane's taken that job. They might be suspicious of me, but around you...those cowboys will talk. Their wives will share. You're safe and accessible. Someone might say more than they intend. Besides, Zane doesn't exactly fit in on that family bench."

"I can't argue with that." She let out a long slow breath and stared at the disguise.

"Isn't this why you came to San Antonio without telling anyone?" Rafe prodded. "To prove yourself?"

"Yeah. And look what I did."

He turned her to face him. "Mallory had a target on her back before you ever arrived, Sierra. At least you were here. You did everything you could to save her. She has a chance, but you're the only witness, and they want you to run. And as far as they know, you have. You checked out, took a cab to the airport and the passenger list shows you're back in Denver."

"Zane?"

"Gotta appreciate what the man can do with records." Rafe picked up the wig. "So, you ready to meet Sarah Vargas, my baby mama?"

She glanced up at Rafe. Her blue eyes held an uncertainty she couldn't hide. "What if I make a mistake?"

"You'll make more than one. The trick is to keep cool and recover." He cupped her cheeks. "Without any other clues, it's the only way that we'll find Mallory and her daughter. You can do this."

Rafe handed her the clothes and pushed her

toward the bathroom. "Oh, and you're Noah Bradford's sister."

He closed the door behind her, and Sierra faced the bathroom mirror. She looked like someone had run a truck over her. Dark circles, pale, tense, bruises blotching her face. How could Rafe think she could do this?

Noah had always been smarter and a way better sneak during his high-school years. He'd lied about his career for years.

Of course, so had she. Noah had done it to protect the family; Sierra had done it so her three brothers and ex-cop dad wouldn't try to stop her.

She leaned forward across the sink and gazed in the mirror. "Where did that woman go?"

With one finger, she tugged her T-shirt away from her left breast and gazed at the infinity-shaped scar. "Damn you, Archimedes," she whispered. She twisted on the faucet, and cold water poured out. She splashed her face.

No time for self-indulgence any longer. Mallory needed her.

Rafe needed her.

If she didn't pull her weight, she could get him killed. She straightened her shoulders and blinked at the woman staring back at her. The woman Sierra saw as vulnerable and weak. She might have played the role, might have challenged Rafe, but it was all an act. The bruise on her cheek and injured thigh proved it.

Not again. Never again.

She pulled off Rafe's sweatpants and T-shirt, but even raising her arms made her ache. She glanced down at her torso. Bruises covered half of her ribs on the right side, another had formed on her thigh. She looked like she'd been through an MMA fight.

With a groan, Sierra slipped into the shower, trying to scrub the aches and sleep away. The water pounded on her back and she winced, twisting, but she couldn't see anything. Finally she stepped out of the stall, dried her hair and slipped into the disguise and new clothes Rafe had provided. Not something she'd normally wear. The dress billowed around her newly round abdomen and fell just below her knees. At least it covered her bruises. The few on her shins she dabbed with makeup to conceal them.

Sierra rummaged through her makeup bag, concealed the facial bruises and finally added a touch of lipstick.

Sarah wouldn't wear a lot of makeup. She was a cowboy's wife.

Finally the hair. She tucked her light brown locks beneath the hairnet and secured the auburn wig.

She held her breath and turned toward the mirror. A stranger stood before her. A very pregnant stranger.

Sierra turned sideways and touched her belly, trapping the dress's fabric against her. It looked too real. With one hand she stroked the mound. Something odd fluttered in her stomach. Weird.

Babies hadn't even been on her radar. Not until her sister-in-law, Emily, had started showing. Mitch's wife had glowed; she'd looked so happy.

Because she was in love.

Sierra had believed herself to be in love. Her night with Rafe had been a good lesson. Lust wasn't love.

She let out a long slow breath. She had to put wishes and dreams out of her mind. She straightened her back and opened the bathroom door.

Rafe stood there like something out of a Western movie. He'd changed into faded blue jeans, a black Western shirt and worn cowboy boots, not his normally black jeans and T-shirt ensemble. His eye patch stood out even more against the white hat. A grin tugged at the corners of his mouth. "Damn, you clean up…real nice." He cleared his throat.

"It looks…real?" she asked.

"All too real." His eyes darkened, and he reached out a tentative hand.

Sierra gave a nervous laugh. "It's just silicone."

He rested his hand on the fake belly. "Too real," he said, then turned from her and dug into his bag. He faced her, holding a small jewelry box. "Give me your left hand," he said softly.

Sierra's entire body trembled. Slowly she raised her arm and stuck out her shaking hand.

Rafe clasped her fingers in his, squeezing them in reassurance. He removed a simple gold band from the velvet holder and slipped it on her finger over her knuckle until it settled there, as if it belonged.

Sierra couldn't breathe. She simply stared. She could barely process what had just happened.

Rafe didn't let go of her hand for a moment, and finally raised his gaze to hers. "It's official," he said, his voice clipped, letting her go and placing a similar band on his own finger. "The single men will take one look at that baby bump and ring and run the other way."

His words shook her out of her daze. The moment was gone. She worried the gold with her finger, fighting to hold back the emotion welling in her chest. She could do this.

"Doesn't say much good about men if this will scare them off."

Rafe paused. "It's a dream for some, a nightmare for others."

"And for you?"

"Both," he said.

Chapter Seven

The winter sun shined with a hazy glow. It heated the interior of the truck. The large arena loomed close. Sierra studied the layout. The rodeo appeared quite different in the afternoon compared to the middle of the night.

Horse trailers and RVs filled a cordoned-off area behind the arena. Rafe pulled into the large parking lot.

"I'm surprised," Sierra said. "Beckel must have gotten his way with the police department. No cops or crime scene tape that I can see."

"Clearly, Beckel knows how to arm-twist the political machine so the rodeo goes off smoothly. It's a big event. Brings a lot of money to the city."

"And if Mallory's discovery put that in jeopardy—"

"A lot of people have a lot to lose."

Sierra's neck and back tensed, and it wasn't

from the extra weight that pressed against her breasts and belly. Her nerves were strung as tight as a rubber band ready to be launched. This had to work.

"It's going to be fine," Rafe said, kneading her shoulder. "We'll get answers, and we'll find them."

"Am I that transparent?"

"Only to me." He slipped the truck into an empty space. "Let's join the rodeo."

He rounded the vehicle and held out his hand to her, threading their fingers. At his touch, electricity shot through her hand. He squeezed tight.

"Don't worry. I've got your back. I promise."

She nodded and pasted on a smile. As they drew closer to the arena's entrance, a tall, lanky man headed across the asphalt to meet them. He was the epitome of a rancher, jeans, Stetson and blue button-down shirt, but strode with purpose, and once he grew closer, Sierra recognized *the look*. He possessed that same edge to him that Rafe and her brother Noah wore.

Ex-military, maybe?

Or something.

He removed his Stetson and reached out his hand. "Rafe Vargas. I thought you'd fallen off the face of the earth. You haven't been out to train with Ironsides in too long."

"J.K. I appreciate you boarding him when I'm away from Carder."

"He's a good one. If you want to breed him, I'd set it up for a fair cut. He's got the barrel racing pedigree to bring you a lot of money."

Rafe tilted his own Stetson back. "I'll think about it."

Sierra looked back and forth between the two men, utterly confused. Was this part of the show, or did they really know each other?

"Your *wife* looks a little out of sorts, Rafe. She okay?"

"*Sarah*, meet Jared King. He's an old and *trusted* friend."

"I know your brother," the rancher said in a low, conspiratorial voice. "I look forward to witnessing his fiancée put a ring on his finger. He needs someone to keep him in line."

So, Jared knew Noah. Did that mean he knew *everything*? The tension at the base of her skull had moved over the back of her head and had settled in her temples. Sierra hoped she could keep up with the subtext of the conversation through the headache.

Jared looked her up and down. "Congratulations are in order, I see." He turned to Rafe. "Pregnancy is a mystery to most men anyway. They'll avoid close scrutiny. Which was obviously your intent."

"Everything is set?" Rafe asked. "You have any trouble?"

"Ransom's check didn't hurt, and the fact that I provide almost a quarter of the rodeo's stock sweetened the deal. But the clincher was your junior rodeo career. John Beckel witnessed a few good bull rides back in the day. He liked your style."

Stunned at this shocking information, Sierra stared at Rafe. "You really *do* ride? I don't know whether to be relieved or terrified. Why didn't you—"

"We'll talk later," Rafe interrupted, closing her open mouth with a bit of pressure from his finger.

He turned to Jared. "Where's my gear?"

"I stowed everything with Ironsides. The preliminaries start in a couple hours. You barely have enough time to get your feet wet."

Rafe stuck out his hand. "I owe you, J.K. Thanks."

"I'll add it to your tab." Jared's face went solemn. "Ransom told me what's at stake. I hope you find what you're looking for. If I can help, just ask." The rancher ambled away, hiking into an old rusted pickup before driving away.

"The guy should get rid of that walking tin bucket, but it's his favorite." Rafe faced her. "You ready to do this?"

"Are you?" Sierra asked. "How long since you've been on a bull?" She didn't know much about the sport, but from the few times she'd caught a glimpse on television, it looked too dangerous to even contemplate.

She frowned at him, but he just smiled and held out his hand to her. "Heck, honey. Bull riding's like riding a bike. The trick is not to lose your balance."

Sierra wasn't so sure.

Rafe waited for her, hand outstretched. She linked her fingers with his, but her stomach rolled. She had a bad feeling about this entire situation.

She didn't know who, but it felt like someone was about to get trampled.

A RODEO POSSESSED A strange combination of odors all its own. She supposed it might appeal to some, but for Sierra, her stomach teetered on rebellion with every step.

Taking a deep swallow and giving her belly a firm lecture, she strode up a ramp with Rafe. They entered the stands surrounding the arena. Seas of faces had pinned their focus on the bucking horse doing its level best to send a cowboy flying.

A shout of enthusiasm followed by a low groan erupted through the stadium.

"The bronc riders are just finishing up."

"I've got to be behind the chute shortly," he whispered. He pointed toward the VIP area behind the chutes. "That's where the wives and families sit. Just relax and get to know them. Trust your instincts."

"This is crazy," she muttered.

He kissed her nose. All for show, she tried to tell herself.

"You can do this. You know why we're here." Linking her hand with his, he escorted her across the arena.

When they arrived, the chattering stopped. Rafe tipped his hat. "Ladies, I wonder if you'd be so kind as to watch over my wife." He patted her belly. "It's her first time."

A few titters filtered across the crowd. Sierra could feel the heat settling in her cheeks.

"I'm Rafe Vargas. This is Sarah."

He held her face between his hands and kissed her lips, slowly, delicately. Her heart did that crazy pitter-patter flip. She was getting too used to his touch. Not a good thing.

"See you later, darlin'. Everything'll be fine."

He walked away and most of the women watched him leave.

"Whoo-wee, that man wears his jeans well," a woman in her midfifties commented. "Gives me a tingle right where it shouldn't."

"Nancy!" one of the women squealed.

Nancy shrugged. "What? Just because I'm a grandma doesn't mean I'm dead from the waist down." She patted the empty space next to her. "Have a seat, darlin'. Before the final round is done day after tomorrow, we'll know all your secrets and probably be able to tell you if that little one you're cookin' is a boy or a girl."

"Don't listen to her, Sarah," a second woman said with a smile. She held out her hand. "I'm Diane Manley. My husband, Travis, rides bulls. Yours?"

"Bulls, too," Sierra said, a tremor in her voice.

"It's where the money is," Diane said. "If he doesn't get hurt."

"And if he can stay on for eight seconds. Six seconds doesn't pay the mortgage," a woman commented, jostling her baby to keep him from crying.

"Or the doctor's bills, April," another chimed in.

"Don't you fret," Nancy said. "I recognize your husband's name. He was one of the best. My man and I have been around this world for three decades. I thought Rafe had smartened up and quit. I guess once rodeo gets in your blood, it's like an infection that keeps comin' back."

The opening was too good to pass up. Sierra ticked through Rafe's instructions. *Tell them just enough to know he has a dubious past and might be for sale.*

She cleared her throat. "Rafe joined the military just after he turned eighteen. That's why he quit."

"A real hero. Good for him." Nancy smiled.

Sierra looked away, dropping her gaze, trying to imitate shame or embarrassment.

"Nancy!" Diane hissed.

She smiled at Sierra. "You don't have to talk about it, Sarah."

With a weak smile, she nodded. "It's okay. I met Rafe after he was discharged. He didn't get retirement, but we make ends meet. He's a good man." She raised her chin in challenge.

A wave of whispering flowed through the crowd. So far so good. Just defensive enough to set up Rafe as a bad boy, but not too much. Hopefully.

"Good for him. And you," Diane said.

"And now, ladies and gentlemen. The event you've all been waiting for. Our Bull Riding Competition!" The announcer's voice poured over the crowd of more than ten thousand. "First up, Travis Manley. Travis is currently tied for second on the leader board." The announcer paused momentarily. "Well, now, today's not this cowboy's lucky day. He's drawn Angel Maker, last year's bull of the year." The crowd gasped. "Never been ridden, folks. Let's hope Travis can break the streak."

Diane turned pale. "Oh no."

"What's wrong?" Sierra whispered to Nancy.

"That bull should be put down. Last year he stomped on one of the riders. Broke his leg, pelvis and a couple bones in his back. That cowboy will never be the same."

Sierra leaned forward, peering down into the bucking chute. A black bull stood still. A lean cowboy lowered himself over the bull and gripped a flat braided rope with a gloved hand.

He nodded once, his face lined with tension. The chute opened, and the moment the bull escaped the enclosure he bucked up, all four hooves leaving the dirt. He twisted right, then left, jerking the cowboy around like a rag doll.

"Travis!" Diane shouted.

The ride seemed to take forever. Angel Maker spun, airborne. The crowd leaped to its feet. The bull switched directions. Travis flew off the side, landing on his back.

Two rodeo clowns ran toward him, hoisting him to his feet and rushing him to the barrier. Angel Maker barreled after them and clipped one of the clowns with his horns. The man stumbled to the ground.

The bull raised up and stomped down.

The crowd shouted in horror. Two men

bounded over the fence and pulled the clown to safety. Sierra recognized Rafe's black Western-style shirt.

The infuriated bull turned his attention to Rafe and charged. Sierra's breath caught in her throat. She twisted her dress in her grip. A gate opened. Rafe raced into it; the bull followed and Rafe vaulted over the fence.

A loud cheer went up.

"How about a round of applause for the latest addition to our competition, folks. Rafe Vargas. He tore up the junior circuit a decade ago, and now he's back. Looks like he's still got some moves." The announcer paused. "A big hand for Travis Manley. He clocked in at 6.8 seconds, ladies and gents. Second best time of the year on Angel Maker."

Sierra sagged in her seat, heart racing. Was Rafe crazy?

"That's some man you caught, girl," Nancy said. "Not bad."

"He's something, all right," Sierra muttered, rising, determined to stop Rafe. She slipped into the aisle. This was too dangerous. There had to be another way.

"Next up, local hero Rafe Vargas. Give it up for the newcomer, folks. He's drawn Sweet Sin."

Sierra froze, her entire body chilled with

fear. Her gaze narrowed. The bull didn't look any less powerful than Angel Maker.

Rafe hovered over the bull and seated himself. He nodded. The chute flew open and the bull rushed out, with Rafe twisting on his back.

A strap encircled the bull's belly, driving the animal to try to buck it off. Time slowed for Sierra. Rafe's body twisted and turned, but his grip remained solid. The animal flailed in the air, and Rafe lost his hold. The bull catapulted him upside down. He hit the dirt hard. The crowd gasped.

A siren blared.

For a moment, Rafe simply lay still. Sierra grabbed the metal railing with a white-knuckle grip.

The beast charged. A clown distracted Sweet Sin, urging the bull out of the arena, leaving Rafe to slowly rise to his feet. He looked into the stands straight at Sierra and lifted his hand to wave to the crowd.

The audience groaned as his score was posted. Zero. "Too bad, folks. Seven seconds for Rafe Vargas. Welcome back, cowboy! Better luck next time."

He could have broken his neck. Sierra's knees shook, her stomach roiled with nausea.

"You okay, darlin'?" Nancy asked. "He done

good for his first ride back, but you look green as an unripened tomato."

"I'll be fine. Maybe a bathroom."

Holding her mouth, Sierra raced up the stairs as quickly as she could.

After she threw up, she'd find Rafe, and she might very well have to kill him.

RAFE'S BOOTS KICKED up dust as he moved away from the chute. He slapped his hat against his jeans. The rodeo hadn't changed, but Rafe had put on ten years. Chasing bad guys and even terrorists didn't use the same muscles as harnessing a two-and-a-half-ton bull.

He weaved through several riders. A couple patted him on the back, and he fought not to wince. His body would be black-and-blue in a couple of days. At least the guys in the ring had kept Sweet Sin from stomping him. Their moniker might be rodeo clowns, but those bullfighters had saved his butt from getting creamed.

One of the men grabbed Rafe as he was leaving the area. "Vargas?"

Rafe stopped. "Yeah?"

"Name's Kurt Prentiss. I—"

"You saved my butt out there." Rafe shook his hand.

Kurt held out a strap. "From Sweet Sin. Thought you should know."

Rafe gave the leather a close look. "Cut?"

The man nodded.

"You know who did it?"

"No, but it's a tight championship this year, and you're changing up the pecking order. It could've been anyone. Most of these guys are too honest for their own good, but there are a few who'll do anything to win...and get their share of the money."

"I'll keep that in mind," Rafe said as Kurt walked away.

Was this about his investigation or simply a rider protecting his position? Just one more element to complicate an already problematic investigation.

Rafe passed by the on-site clinic and winced at the bullfighter who'd bailed out Travis Manley lying on a stretcher.

The bull rider hovered outside the entrance.

"How is he?" Rafe asked Travis.

"Hopefully they can pin him back together. He's one of the best." Travis scowled. "I should've moved faster. My neck's been acting up, and the blow stunned me." He studied Rafe. "You had a good ride for just getting back into it. Word's already spread about your national championship."

"A decade ago. I was a kid," Rafe said, rubbing his own neck. "It's not the same. Hurts more this time around."

"That's for sure. Think we had rubber bones back then?"

"Or we were so jacked up on adrenaline we never felt it." Rafe paused. "Travis, what do you make of this?" He handed over the strap.

Rafe knew the cowboy was running second. He had a motive. Rafe wanted to see his reaction.

"Holy—" The expletive exploded. "Where'd you get this?"

"It's the strap from my ride," Rafe said.

Travis's face went white. "This was done on purpose. If it had snapped…"

"I know. Any idea who it might've been?"

Something in Rafe's tone must've clued Travis in. He crossed his arms. "You thought it might be me."

"You're in second place. You have something to gain."

"Not when I draw that damn Angel Maker and can't make my ride."

Rafe had survived a decade in covert and black ops by counting on his instincts. He trusted them. He had to, and he didn't believe Travis had been involved. His shock had been genuine. "I don't think you cut the strap, but I wonder if you've heard any scuttlebutt about someone—"

"So desperate to win they'd be willing to kill," Travis finished. "You just arrived. It's an awfully quick leap."

"Maybe they weren't willing to take any chances." Rafe met Travis's gaze. "If anything strange crosses your path, would you let me know? Whoever did this to me might do it to someone else."

Travis nodded, his frown deepening, his expression contemplative.

The roar of the crowd boomed even through the bowels behind the arena. Rafe rounded the corner and walked straight into a skinny figure propped up against the wall of the clinic. A tingling of awareness shot down Rafe's neck.

"Tough fall," the man said.

He had the wiry frame of a rider, but didn't appear strong enough.

"I'll survive." Rafe tilted his Stetson back to study the man who'd stopped him.

"You're gonna be hurtin' tomorrow. I might be able to help."

Now the guy had Rafe's interest. "Really? How? Magic beans?"

"Kind of. The docs here'll give you pills if you got insurance or the money to pay out of pocket. Most don't. I got the same stuff. We get it online from out of the country at a bargain."

"You trying to sell me sugar pills?" Rafe commented. "Not interested."

He edged around the man, but the guy grabbed Rafe's shirt. "It's the good stuff. I got customers who can vouch for me. My supplier's legit."

Prescription drugs. The rodeo circuit moved from town to town. Not a bad cover for dealing. Selling the drugs and laundering money through the rodeo made a lot of sense.

"Keep talking," Rafe said. "I can't afford insurance right now, and with my wife having a baby, we're strapped for cash."

"You won't make it tomorrow after that head dive."

"I don't have the money on me," Rafe lied, giving a concerned look around, as if he were nervous someone would see them. "Meet me later? After hours?"

The man studied him, then offered a brief nod. "Sure. Make yourself visible at the end of the day, and I'll find you."

Rafe leaned closer, pretended to lose his balance and jostled the dealer.

"Whoa, dude. Back off."

Rafe swayed. "Sorry. Guess that fall hit my head more than I thought." He walked away, taking care not to look back, then ducked down an aisle lined with stalls. Keeping out of sight, he surveyed the dealer and tapped his phone.

"Mom, is that you?" Zane asked.

"I take it you're not alone," Rafe commented. "I've got a target on the west side of the rodeo's medical clinic. He's dealing. I tried picking his pocket, but no wallet, only pills and cash. I need you to run his prints for an ID, but I couldn't risk lifting the drug package for testing. He'd be suspicious of me when he noticed them missing."

"I can do that, Mom. Milk and eggs. I'll have them to the house as soon as I can."

"Thanks, Zane."

Waiting for his CTC backup to take over, Rafe kept his prey under surveillance. He had half a mind to grab the guy and beat the tar out of him, but one hint of the net closing around the kidnapper's plans could cost Mallory and Chloe their lives. This operation had to be completed covertly and subtly.

He tugged out his phone, keeping the dealer in his line of sight.

You okay? he texted.

Turn around.

Sierra stood behind him, arms crossed. She stalked over to him and slugged him in the solar plexus.

He let out a loud oomph. "What was that for?"

"You scared me. You executed a swan dive headfirst into the dirt. You could've been hurt, or paralyzed or…" Sierra's jaw pulsed. "Don't do it again."

Rafe tilted his head. "I've taken more dangerous assignments."

She gnawed at her lip. "It's one thing to read the reports. It's another to…watch."

"I'm fine." With a glance around at several very interested faces, he walked her to the side, out of earshot of the cowboys and rodeo staff wandering in and out of the stalls, but keeping his target in view.

Unfortunately, he met the guy's gaze. The drug dealer smiled and tipped his hat. Damn. He'd seen Rafe with Sierra. He didn't want that scumbag to have her on his radar. It put her in danger. He'd give anything if she'd leave, but they were all in now.

At that moment Sierra swayed against him.

He wrapped his arm around her waist. "Are you okay? You look pale. Like you're going to pass out."

"I've just thrown up everything I've eaten in the last twenty-four hours," she said. "Burritos don't look nearly as appetizing going up. The good news is getting sick at watching your neck bend in ways it wasn't meant to solidified my undercover identity. Everyone believes I'm pregnant, that's for sure."

He studied her, trying to see through her lies.

"I promise. I'll get used to the odor. Eventually."

"Did you overhear anything suspicious?"

"A few wives complaining about money and mortgages, but not much else. And nothing about Mallory and Chloe." She let out a long sigh. "Is this going to work? Are we any closer to finding them, because I don't see it."

"Everything we've discovered points to the money. The cops agree. According to Cade, the San Antonio police are still looking at Mallory as an embezzlement suspect."

"Idiots. Can't they see the truth?" She pressed her lips together.

He really didn't like the look of her. "You're *sure* you're not coming down with something."

"I'm fine. Just worried."

"Well, too many are watching, so I guess we play the part of a newly married couple for a few minutes." Rafe cupped her face and lowered his lips, capturing her gasp.

She tasted of minty toothpaste, and her warm lips parted under his. She clutched at his shirt, and all he could think about was whisking her away, to someplace safe.

Behind them a horse snorted. Footsteps

clomped closer. Rafe tensed and raised his head. He turned, placing himself between Sierra and the unwelcome visitor.

"Rafe Vargas." A man in his sixties tilted his hat back and raked his gaze from Rafe to Sierra. "You've stirred up quite a bit of excitement at my rodeo. You've got the bull riders talking, which doesn't happen often. So I gotta wonder, are you the kind of man who brings excitement or the wrong kind of trouble with you?"

Chapter Eight

Mallory lay flat on her belly. Tall buffalo grass surrounded her and Chloe like a thin, wispy curtain swaying in the breeze. No protection, merely concealment. Mallory's face dripped with sweat. Huddled next to her mother, Chloe sobbed quietly beside her.

"Where did she go?" The cop shouted from across the small meadow.

Mallory recognized his voice. She'd never forget it as long as she lived.

He let loose a flurry of curses. "Everyone backtrack. Try the other path. Failure isn't an option. The boss won't forgive. Or forget."

The cop wasn't the boss? Mallory's mind whirled in confusion. Then who was? How many people were involved?

Several sets of footsteps stomped away accompanied by muttering complaints. She waited until the sounds disappeared in the distance. Then waited several minutes longer.

When she was certain they'd gone, Mallory dropped her forehead against the dirt. Her lungs ached, and for the first time, she realized she'd been holding her breath. She gasped for air.

"Mommy?"

"Shh, Button."

Ever so slowly Mallory sat up. The sky had begun to darken, but it would take a couple hours for night to fall. They weren't safe here. If those men came back, it would be all too easy to stumble over their hiding place.

She squinted through the dim light. A few thousand yards away, a thick patch of forest erupted out of the prairie grass. The trees could hide them until Mallory figured out which way to go to get to civilization and find a phone for help.

She rose to her knees and turned in a circle, searching for another option, any sign of a road or trail, a house or a barn, but only a second patch of forest dotted the horizon, even farther away. And in the same direction the men had hiked.

Easy choice. Everything inside her told her to stay as far away from that cop as possible. Her mind made up, she held out her hand to

Chloe. "Let's go, Button. We're making a run for those trees."

"It's too far. I'm hungry. And thirsty."

"I know, sweetie. I'll find you something. Soon."

Chloe thrust out her jaw and folded her arms across her chest. "No. I'm tired. I don't want to go. I want my house and Princess Buttercup."

Mallory sighed, sat back and pulled her daughter onto her lap. "I know you're exhausted, honey. So am I. But we have to keep going. Or we'll have to go back to the trailer."

Chloe's eyes widened with fear. "I don't want to go there. It smelled funny, and that man took you away from me."

Choking back a sob, Mallory closed her eyes and hugged her daughter close. "You ready?" she whispered. "We have to be brave like Sierra."

"She can run fast."

"That she can."

Mallory stood and clasped Chloe's hand.

They ran. Sweat dripped down Mallory's cheeks. The trees grew closer and closer. Mallory's feet pounded on the grasslands, her steps small so Chloe could keep up.

Only a few dozen feet more.

"We're almost there," she panted, speeding up as much as she could.

Mallory's foot sank down. She pitched forward. A sharp pain shot through her ankle and foot. She slammed to the ground on hands and knees.

"Mommy!" Chloe skidded to a halt and fell beside her mother.

Sucking in breath after breath, Mallory froze. Her leg throbbed. She rolled over. Agony shot from her foot to her knee. White spots danced in front of her eyes. The light dimmed.

Don't pass out. Don't pass out.

She stared up at the purple sky, a smattering of stars beginning to shine through. She tried to focus, and finally her head stopped spinning. She sat up and shifted her leg, biting her lip to keep from crying out in pain.

"Mommy?" Chloe's voice was small and scared.

Mallory folded her daughter to her chest. Off to the direction they'd come from, through the dim light, she caught a glimpse of several flashlight beams sweeping back and forth.

Her heart sank. If they saw the signs, they'd follow them here.

"It'll be fine, Button," she lied. "We're going to be just fine."

TROUBLE. MORE THAN one person had accused Rafe of being exactly that through the years.

He didn't like being cornered, or attacked. He tended to fight back with lethal force.

As if she'd read his mind, Sierra squeezed Rafe's shoulder, her touch restraining him from uttering the choice phrases he would surely regret. He quelled his temper. This operation required finesse, not firepower.

No wonder he preferred attacking from stealth. Wham, bam, done was much more his style.

He forced a smile on his face. "No trouble from me, Mr. Beckel. I just appreciate the invitation to participate." Rafe tugged Sierra forward and pressed her against his side. "We appreciate the helping hand. Sarah and I aim to start a new life."

John Beckel stuffed a pinch of tobacco between his cheek and lower lip. He gave them both a hard stare. "Well, Jared King vouched for you, and that man knows his stock and his riders. Besides, everyone's entitled to a mistake," the rodeo owner said. "Lord knows I've married six of them. Much to my brother Warren's irritation. They're bleeding me dry. That's why I gotta keep this place out of trouble and profitable. You catch my drift, boy?"

Rafe nodded, making a note to have Zane run background checks on Beckel's exes. He'd known the rodeo's finances were tight, but now he understood one reason why. "From everything I've heard, sir, you run a well-oiled machine. That's why I picked this event to try for my comeback."

John frowned. "I *thought* I had everything under control. Until yesterday. Sometimes people surprise you. You think you know a person… I hired her, trusted her. I guess that's why I've got six exes."

Sierra leaned forward, pressing her hand against his arm. "I'm so sorry, Mr. Beckel."

He patted her hand, his eyes softening as his gaze scraped up and down Sierra's disguise. "Don't be sorry for me, young lady, be sorry for my bank account. Speaking of which, I've got a new office manager I'm breaking in. Jared King recommended him, too, but between you and me, I'm not sure he belongs in an office. I need to keep an eye on him."

Rafe held back a smile of satisfaction. Zane must be playing his part well.

"Good luck tomorrow, Vargas. If you ride well…we'll see what I can do for you. And your lovely wife." He stretched out his hand.

Rafe shook it. "It's been nice to meet you, sir. I'll do my best not to disappoint."

If Rafe were the suspicious type, which he was, he'd wonder exactly what hidden message

John Beckel had just communicated. Zane definitely needed to do some research.

John tipped his hat. He was just turning to leave when Rafe noticed Zane's figure flashing past the entrance to the row of stalls over John's shoulder. Damn. Zane was heading to the drug dealer to get those prints. They couldn't afford for John to see Zane away from the office.

Rafe stepped forward. "Sir. Would you care to see my horse? Jared trains him. Ironsides is a barrel racer. I'll be riding him in the closing ceremony on the final day of the rodeo."

John paused. "Some other time, maybe," he said with a quizzical look. "After my assistant's embezzlement, I don't want to leave the office for too long. Not for a while anyway."

Nothing for Rafe to do, but let him go.

Sierra leaned up against him. "Zane made it," she whispered in his ear. "He gave me a thumbs-up. He'll beat Beckel back to his office."

Dodged a bullet that time. "Good. We'll touch base at the hotel tonight. Hopefully he'll have our smoking gun after spending all day on that computer."

Rafe gripped Sierra's elbows and gave her the once-over. "Now, back to our previous conversation. Are you really okay?"

"How many times do I have to tell you? It's fine. I'm fine. Feeling better with every minute that passes, actually. Maybe my sense of smell has been deadened," she said.

"And your leg?"

"Almost as good as new. When are you going to stop asking?"

"When I'm convinced you're telling the truth," he muttered.

"Are you this much of a mother hen with all your partners?"

"The few partners I've had don't start the mission with a bullet wound."

She twisted her lip. "Point," she said, her tone frustrated.

An awkward pause settled between them. She smoothed her dress over her silicone belly. "I know you don't want me here," she started.

"It worries me. I don't want you hurt. I care…" He let his words die off.

She reached for his hand. "Can I meet Iron-sides?"

The eyebrow over Rafe's good eye arched. Not since his brother and his foster dad had anyone shown a real interest in Rafe's passion for horses. "You really want to?"

"Something in your expression when you mentioned him made me curious."

"Come on, then." He guided her to the stall where Jared King had housed Ironsides. The large quarter horse whinnied softly.

The mahogany coat shined and the rabicano markings just above his hooves reminded her of white socks. "He's beautiful," Sierra said.

Rafe opened the gate. He walked inside and patted the side of the horse's neck. "Bet you never thought we'd be here, huh?" he whispered.

He led the horse closer to Sierra. "Meet Ironsides. Best barrel racer off the rodeo circuit." The horse nuzzled Rafe's pocket. "Sorry, boy. Nothing for you today."

"With a name like Ironsides, I expected him to be gray," Sierra said, stroking his nose.

"He's called Ironsides because he was about to be put out to pasture before his time, just like the ship," Rafe said. "He'd been neglected, and the local vet in Carder thought he might have to be destroyed. I asked if I could to take him and try to rehabilitate him. He still had some fight left."

Ironsides nudged Rafe forward.

"I think he's telling you that you should've brought a carrot or two."

"You know horses?"

Sierra shook her head. "I took a few lessons when I went to summer camp, but the closest I got to serious riding was attending the rodeo with M...my best friend."

"Good catch, in case someone's listening," he said softly in her ear.

The scent of her shampoo encompassed him.

If he lowered his head just a bit, and she turned hers, he could kiss her again.

Instead, he straightened and rubbed her back. "I'll get Ironsides bedded down, and we'll return to the motel. Hopefully our friend has some news."

He'd have preferred to take her to *his* home and lock her up so he'd be certain she was protected. But Rafe couldn't take her to a place that didn't exist. His home was the occasional motel, and a piece of land near Carder, Texas, that he'd purchased on a whim. An empty piece of land with nothing on it but rattlesnakes, cacti and some very valuable copper and mineral rights.

Ironsides shifted back and forth. When he stepped on his right front leg, his gait looked off. "What's wrong, boy?"

Rafe knelt and ran his finger along the limb, feeling for the telltale signs of a tendon or ligament injury.

"Your horse have a problem?" a voice asked from behind.

Rafe turned his head to see a solidly built man with a crew cut leaning against the gate next to Sierra.

"I'm Harlen Anderson. The rodeo vet. Good-looking mount."

Standing, Rafe rested his hand against Ironsides's neck. "Rafe Vargas. My wife, Sarah.

And this is Ironsides. He's a good one all right. But he might have a strained tendon."

"Ma'am." Harlen tipped his hat. "Want me to take a look?"

Rafe opened the gate. "I'd appreciate it."

Maybe their luck was changing. In addition to helping Ironsides, someone like Harlen would know practically everyone involved with the rodeo.

The vet moved slowly from limb to limb, taking his time. "Saw your ride, Vargas. Sweet Sin is no easy bull. You held your own."

"Seven seconds doesn't pay the bills," Rafe said with a frown. He ran his hand down Ironsides's flank. "I may have to start entering more events. Especially with the baby coming. Or get a part-time job."

"I'll keep my ears open," Harlen said. He stood. "That right front leg has a bit of edema, but it's not too bad. Cold compresses and rest should take care of it. I have one in my office that'll do the trick."

"Thanks." Rafe stroked Ironsides's flank. "Hear that boy? The doc's gonna fix you up as good as new."

"Don't mention it. I'll be back in a few minutes."

The vet strode away, and Rafe followed his exit with a speculative gaze.

"I know that look." Sierra leaned forward against the gate. "He seemed nice enough to me. What do you see?"

"Maybe nothing. But he came out of nowhere at the exact moment I noticed the injury."

"Coincidence?"

The moment the words were out, Rafe met Sierra's gaze. "There's no such thing as a coincidence," they said over each other.

"Ransom taught you well." Rafe let a small smile twist his lips. "It's the truth, though. I can count on one finger the times a coincidence was truly just chance."

"Actually it was Noah," Sierra said. "I was about thirteen, and my bicycle tire went flat. Joey Malone *happened* to be nearby to walk me home and steal my first kiss.

"That was probably my first lecture from Noah, but definitely not my last."

"I might've done the same thing." Rafe touched her cheek lightly, relishing the feel of her smooth skin. Did he imagine she leaned into his touch? Was it wishful thinking?

Sierra chewed on her lip for a moment. "If Dr. Anderson showing up wasn't a coincidence, what was it? He was watching us and decided just to say hi? Why? What's his interest?"

Rafe grabbed a brush and began to groom

Ironsides. "Excellent question. I don't know, but we just added another name to our suspect list."

DARKNESS HAD LONG since settled over San Antonio when Sierra entered the motel room, her feet weary, her mind disheartened. Her shoulders had tensed up, her breasts ached and her back hurt from carrying the extra weight on her belly.

Princess Buttercup sauntered over to the door, passed by Zane without pause and stared unflinchingly at Rafe. He shook his head at the feline. "I'll do a quick perimeter sweep." He closed the door behind him with a firm click.

Princess Buttercup swished her tail at the door, but didn't move. Simply stared and sat down. Waiting.

"That cat's spooky," Zane said. "She's waiting for him."

"It took me a half dozen trips for her to warm up to me," Sierra said. "The princess fell for Rafe in five minutes."

Not unlike Sierra.

She raised her arms and stretched. The cat wouldn't move until Rafe returned. "I don't even want to bother taking this thing off," Sierra groaned, taking a straight shot to the bed and flopping back on it.

She simply lay there staring at the ceiling.

Zane chuckled. "How does it feel to be knocked up?"

"You try it sometime." She gave him that look her brothers had nicknamed her Sierra-stink-eye. "You know what the worst part is? This stupid thing gave me sympathy symptoms. I couldn't keep breakfast or lunch down."

Zane scanned her. "Now that's spooky."

The key turned in the lock. Zane and Sierra both palmed their weapons within seconds when Rafe stepped through the door.

He arched a brow. "We're clear. The owner didn't see anyone suspicious hanging around today. We're good. For now."

He knelt down and scratched Princess Buttercup behind the ears. The cat purred, butted his hand, then returned to the towel he'd arranged for her in the corner of the motel room, circled and settled down, staring at them all.

Rafe's gaze lasered in on Sierra's reclining body. "What's wrong?"

"I'm f—"

"Don't say you're fine, when you're clearly not."

"I'm tired. Nothing a hot shower and a few acetaminophen won't cure."

Rafe leaned over the bed, practically nose to nose with her. "I don't like the look of you."

She pushed herself up. "You're not getting me to go back to Carder, Rafe. I made contacts today. Mallory and Chloe have been gone over twenty-four hours. We're running out of time. We all know that after seventy-two hours, their chances of survival decrease to practically nothing."

"Yes, but you won't help anyone if you can't focus," Rafe argued, not moving an inch, forcing himself into her space.

She refused to back down from his challenge. "If you want to help, why not hand me my computer so I don't have to get up." She gave him a sweet-as-licorice smile. "Zane and I work faster together."

Zane glanced between Sierra and Rafe with a wide grin on his face.

"What?" Rafe turned to his friend and barked. "You have information to share that will catch these kidnappers?"

The man frowned. "Someday you'll have to ask me about what I saw between the two of you, but for now, I can give you a report."

He opened up his laptop, lowered his large frame into one of the chairs and moved a nightstand to create a makeshift table. Within a few minutes, he'd pulled out a secure satellite link and his fingers flew across the keyboard.

"What's the access IP address?" Sierra asked, relieved when Rafe stood and crossed the room. The farther away from her he was, the better. He was too much of a distraction.

Zane rattled off a series of numbers, and Sierra used her secure token to log in to CTC's private network.

Sierra quickly ran a few queries against the names of the women she'd met in the VIP section.

While she and Zane worked the ones and zeroes, Rafe propped himself up against the door. "I met with our drug dealer today. His name is Curtis Lawson, and he goes by Spider. But only to his friends."

"Seriously?" Zane's fingers paused. "If I were a criminal, I wouldn't pick the name of an insect most people step on."

Rafe shrugged and pulled a packet of five pills from his pocket. "He sold me what he claims is oxycodone. I'm rendezvousing with Detective Cade Foster later tonight. He'll have it tested."

Zane tapped a couple more keys. "While you two were keeping the boss busy—thanks, by the way—I was able to offer 'Spider' a cold drink and grab his prints."

"And?"

"His name *isn't* Curtis Lawson, it's Curtis Leighton. He's got a long juvenile record starting when his mother remarried. He grew up in Houston with one stepsister. I haven't had a chance to go down that path yet, but he doesn't seem like the type who'd have a lot of sisterly love, so it's probably a dead end."

"And you'll check her out anyway." Rafe sounded so certain Sierra didn't know why he'd even mentioned it.

"Of course. Which brings us to my boss, John Beckel."

Zane relayed what he'd discovered, most of which Sierra and Rafe knew. Until Zane started in on the ex-wives.

"Here's where it gets interesting. He's been late on his alimony payments the last couple of months. I count him as our most viable suspect at the moment. He has the means, motive and the opportunity, but he's also pretty clueless when it comes to computers and accounting." Zane sent Sierra a long, slow look. "He didn't do this alone. He needed help."

"What about his brother, the silent partner?" Rafe asked. "Could he be involved?"

"I don't see how. He doesn't have access to any of the systems. From what I can tell, he's more of the marketing and investing arm of the corporation. The last couple years, Warren gave John over a hundred grand to keep the rodeo afloat. While Warren seems to have the magic touch when it comes to business, John doesn't have that gift. He focuses on the rodeo alone, but Warren has a lot of fingers in a lot of pies."

"John doesn't sound like someone who's laundering millions if he needs his brother's help," Rafe muttered. "Can you tell who *does* have access to the computer system?"

Zane let out a long sigh. "Mallory Harrigan and John Beckel were the only ones with passwords until I came on board."

Sierra shook her head. "Mallory wouldn't do this, and she wouldn't make the mistakes I saw in that ledger. I think the mistakes were a signal to me. It *wasn't* her. I can feel it."

Zane shook his head slowly, and Sierra could see he didn't believe her. Then again why should he? She had no proof. Just her gut.

"If Mallory helped him," Zane said, "he could pin the crime on her, write off the loss and collect the insurance money." He cracked his knuckles. "Sorry, sugar, but your friend doesn't look all that innocent right now."

Sierra sagged into the pillow. She raised her gaze to Rafe. "I know it looks bad, but after everything she's been through, she would never risk Chloe this way."

Rafe sat on the bed beside Sierra. "I know you believe that, but Mallory keeps coming back into our line of investigation."

"Which is why they kidnapped her," Sierra said. "Maybe it really is her ex."

"Now there's an interesting possibility. Did you know Bud Harrigan got Mallory the job at the rodeo in the first place?" Zane asked. "He knows the Beckel brothers."

"From where? Is he on the rodeo's payroll?" Sierra couldn't imagine a toad like Bud having anything in common with the owner of the rodeo. They didn't travel in the same circles.

"Not on the legitimate books. I haven't found a second set yet."

"Bud Harrigan's getting more and more smelly. The more we learn about him, the more I want to have a serious conversation with this guy." Rafe drummed his fingers on the bed. "Find him, Zane."

Sierra wouldn't want to be on the receiving end of that interrogation. Rafe's expression had darkened as if he had prey in his sights.

Rafe's jaw throbbed. "I may have been wrong," he said. "I didn't think he had a motive to abduct his family, but if he's involved with the twenty-five million, that's a definite game changer."

Chapter Nine

Darkness surrounded Sierra. She didn't want to open her eyes. She didn't want to remember. A heavy weight pressed on her chest and stomach.

Confused, she reached down and touched the silicone disguise. Then she remembered. Mallory. Chloe. What was she doing falling asleep? They needed her.

Sierra had a bad feeling. Something ominous niggled at the back her of brain.

The soft click of a door closing caused Sierra's eyes to snap open. A rectangle of light shined through the door.

Her hand gripped the Glock.

"It's just me," Rafe said in a low voice. He flipped on one of the bedside lamps. "You're still dressed?"

She rubbed her eyes. "I fell asleep. Guess I was more tired than I thought."

In truth, she hadn't moved since Rafe left.

"How'd your meeting with Cade go?" she asked.

"I delivered the oxycodone. Their lab will do the testing, and he'll get back to me. Maybe they can tell its origins from the formulation. We'll see." Rafe scanned the room. "Where's Zane?"

"He was tired of Princess Buttercup pouting and staring at the door, so he's holed up in his room with his computer." Sierra pushed up, fighting back a yawn "Exactly what I should be doing."

Rafe sat on the side of the bed. "You didn't sleep much last night. You need the rest." He clasped her hand in his. "Mallory and Chloe need you at your best. We won't find them by strength or force. We both know that. It's going to take a mistake on the kidnapper's part, and us being smarter than him."

Sierra wanted to argue, but with Zane working his magic, she knew Rafe was right. Her brain was foggy. She could barely put two thoughts together. "You'll wake me early?"

Rafe nodded. "Of course."

She stood and shrugged her aching shoulders before plodding to the bathroom. The lock snicked closed behind her, and she lifted the flowing dress over her head. Letting it drop to the floor, she tried to unhook the back of the prosthetic, but she couldn't reach it.

After several minutes of trying, she finally gave up. She held the dress in front of her and stuck her head out of the bathroom.

"Rafe?" she said softly.

He'd pulled out his own laptop. He shut the lid and peered at her with a quizzical look.

"I need some help."

His Adam's apple bobbed, but he stood and walked over. She backed away from the door.

"I can't get it off."

"Turn around," he said, his voice husky.

He unhooked the straps and laid the silicone contraption on the counter. She held the dress in front of her chest, not wanting him to look at Archimedes's symbol on the upper curve of her left breast. Not that Rafe hadn't seen it when he'd rescued her. And again when they'd made love. But the scar reminded her every day of her vulnerability. Her own weakness. She'd allowed the serial killer to get the drop on her.

Still, she hated that Rafe would be reminded of her failure. How could it not diminish her in his eyes?

"You don't have to hide from me, you know," he said softly, handing her the thin, silk robe she'd placed on the hook behind the door. "To me it's a badge of courage…and survival."

Rafe's heated look made her cheeks burn. Turning her back to him, she quickly wrapped the robe around her and tightened the belt.

"Come with me and lie down." He held out his hand to her. "I need to clean your wound. It's overdue," he ordered, his voice low.

She perched on the edge of the bed while he disappeared into the bathroom. He returned with a towel and the medical supplies Sierra had purchased yesterday.

"Lie down," he repeated.

With a deep breath, she reclined on the bed. The robe rode up her leg, but it didn't matter, because Rafe would've pushed the material aside anyway.

He eased the tape off and removed the bandage, but some of the gauze stuck to the wound. All that walking had caused it to bleed.

When he tugged, she winced.

"Sorry," he said, grimacing. "I know it hurts."

"Just get it done," she said, closing her eyes, looking away from him, staring at the motel's closet, trying to concentrate on anything but what he was doing.

"First time I bandaged up a leg, I worked on my first horse. A mare named Daisy."

If he'd seen her face, he would have witnessed her surprise. "You had a horse named Daisy? I never would have guessed."

"Not my choice of moniker."

Princess Buttercup pounced on the bed and watched Rafe intently. "Don't give me that look, P.B.," he said. "You have water and food and a place to sleep. Deal with it."

"P.B.?" Sierra asked.

"I'm not calling that cat Princess Buttercup. It's a bigger blow to my masculinity and reputation than Daisy, and I shortened her name to 'D' when my last foster father gave her to me. Best horse on his ranch."

She chanced a glance over her shoulder.

He soaked a pad of gauze with antiseptic and met her gaze. "Take a breath. This could sting."

Rafe bent over her thigh. The moment the liquid touched her open wound she couldn't bite back the gasp.

She shut her eyes tightly. "How long did you live on a ranch?" she squeaked, trying to distract herself.

He didn't respond immediately, but swabbed her injury instead. Would he answer? Rafe rarely spoke about his past.

He let out a long, slow breath. "I moved to the ranch when I was about thirteen. I hated that man when he took me in. Hell, I hated the world."

The burning dissipated, and Sierra opened her eyes, stunned at the revelation.

"What happened to you, Rafe?"

"Still prickling?" he asked, ignoring her question.

"I'll survive."

He dried the wound. Every touch needled her skin. The injury was only a little over a day old. "If you just quit touching me and leave me alone, you won't hurt me," she muttered.

His pointed gaze from his good eye pinned her to the pillow. "Unfortunately, there's nothing I can do about that. I'm going to hurt you."

Suddenly she got the distinct impression they were no longer speaking about the bullet graze, but of the tension that had been smoldering between them, increasing in intensity with each hour they'd spent together.

She clenched the bedspread with her hands. "Just get it over with."

Her gut tightened with anticipation. She stared at his steady hands while he proceeded to squeeze antibiotic ointment on a clean gauze. His hand hovered over her wound.

Sierra couldn't stop her leg from flinching, and he hadn't even touched her yet.

Rafe placed his warm hand on her thigh to hold her down. "I was eleven when my parents died in a car wreck." Very gently he wiped the thick gel across the injury. "My brother, Michael, was sixteen. We had no relatives. Child Protective Services couldn't find anyone who would take in a teenager and an angry eleven-year-old who acted out. We ran away. Michael tried to take care of me, but he fell into the wrong crowd to make money. He was shot selling drugs to feed us. I was shoved into the system and labeled as incorrigible. I decided to prove them right and ran away from a half dozen foster homes when they set me up with Old Man Lancaster. He was my last chance.

"Better?" he asked, avoiding her gaze.

"Yes." She didn't know what else to say. He'd given her the facts of his life in such a matter-of-fact tone, but anyone with a heart could see beyond the words. Rafe had lived a childhood of loss.

"Good."

She wanted to pull him close to her, to hug him tight, but the stiffness of his body stopped her from even reaching out a hand to him.

Rafe stood, gathered the supplies and disappeared into the bathroom.

"What did Mr. Lancaster do that convinced you to stay?"

"He treated me like he expected me to stay, to work, to be a part of his family. He treated me like a son," Rafe said, returning to her side and lowering the robe to cover her upper thigh.

"And he taught you to ride bulls," she surmised.

"First he instructed me how to ride a horse. Then barrel racing. I'm the one who picked bulls when I was sixteen. He didn't want me to go that direction, but I had a knack."

Sierra's heart ached for the young boy Rafe had been. Completely alone until he'd found his foster father, the ranch and the rodeo. He could so easily have taken another path.

"From what the rodeo wives said, you haven't lost your touch. They think you could win the whole thing if you rode full-time."

Rafe rubbed his neck and popped a couple of anti-inflammatories. "I'm way past my prime, honey."

Sierra bit her lip when he swallowed the pills. "You scared me today," she admitted. She'd been angry before, but alone, in the dim light of this room, the gut-wrenching terror that had frozen her when he'd flown through the air head over heels off that bull came back.

"We're getting closer. I may not even have to ride tomorrow. If we can find Mallory's ex and he's responsible, this could all be over."

Rafe cupped her cheeks. The long lashes of his eye blinked. Sierra's heart thudded, its pace quickening. She could barely breathe with him this close.

His thumb ran across her lower lip. He bent closer. "I want to kiss you," he said in a deep voice, low and urgent.

She licked her lips and he let out a low groan, not waiting any longer. His mouth parted hers, and Sierra wrapped her arms around him.

Sinking back against the pillow, she pulled him with her. He pressed one jean-clad leg between hers, arching his hips, giving her no doubt how much he wanted her.

They shouldn't do this, but Sierra's heart and body didn't want to listen to her mind. She wanted to feel Rafe again. She wanted him to love her.

Love her.

She froze. Her heart sank.

Rafe lifted his lips. "What's wrong? Did I hurt you?"

"Not yet, but you will." She shifted out from under him and sat up on the bed. "I want more than anything to lose myself in your arms tonight, but I can't do this again, Rafe." She lifted her chin. "I want more."

He sucked in a shuddering breath. His hands trembled when he touched her hair. "You deserve more," he said, his voice low and gravelly. "You deserve everything."

He rose from the bed. "Get some rest, Sierra. I'll be watching over you."

With those words, he flipped the lock on the motel room door and walked outside into the night.

Sierra buried her head in the pillow. Tears slid down her cheeks. Somewhere deep inside she'd hoped he'd say that he wanted more, too. That he wanted love and a family and forever.

Princess Buttercup let out a soft meow and burrowed her body next to Sierra, as if sensing her shattered heart.

"I should have known, P.B.," she whispered into the fur. "I should have known."

MALLORY SCOOTED ON her belly a few more inches. Her hands and knees stung. She didn't know how long it had taken to reach the edge of the grove of trees. Darkness had long since taken hold. She could see nothing around her but pitch-black darkness.

Her foot throbbed with each heartbeat, but she had to keep inching forward.

"Chloe?" she whispered.

Her daughter sniffled, her small fist tugging against her mother's shirt.

"Just a little farther, Button."

Only a few stars shined overhead, and the

sliver of moonlight was diffused by cloud cover, making it even darker.

Good for hiding, not so good for seeing where you were going.

Mallory reached forward. Her hand banged against the trunk of a tree. She gripped the ground cover and pushed herself up until she was leaning back against the cottonwood.

"Mommy, are you okay?"

Not by a long shot.

"I'm fine. I just twisted my ankle."

An owl hooted. Chloe hunkered down next to her mother.

"I'm scared."

"Me, too, sweetie."

Mallory squinted her eyes and searched the darkness surrounding her. No sounds of men shouting or flashlights or dogs. Had they given up for the night?

Maybe.

She tried moving her leg, but her ankle screamed in pain. If she couldn't walk, how was she supposed to protect Chloe?

Mallory shifted up to her knees, holding her foot off the ground so as not to jostle it. She grabbed the trunk and leaned on it.

"Let's play hide-and-seek, Button."

"It's dark. I can't see anything," Chloe whimpered. "I'm scared."

Mallory rounded one tree and with her hands felt for another. When she encountered wood, she rose on one leg, keeping her weight off her foot and hopped toward the second tree. By the time she'd reached what she'd hoped was the middle of the dense forest, she couldn't even see the stars and moon above. This would have to do.

She stretched above her and grabbed a branch, stripping the leaves off to create a makeshift weapon. It wasn't much, but it was all she had.

Sweating and exhausted, she sank to the ground, leaned up again the tree and patted her lap.

"Lie down, Button. Try to get some sleep."

Her own stomach rumbled.

"Are you hungry, too, Mommy?" Chloe asked with a whimper.

"No, honey," she lied. "My stomach's just talking to me."

"My tummy's saying it's really, really hungry."

"I know."

"When the sun wakes up, can we leave?"

Mallory gripped the stick tight, leaned her head against the rough bark and sent up a silent prayer she'd hidden them well enough to survive another night.

"I hope so, Button. I really hope so."

MORNING LIGHT HADN'T improved Rafe's disposition after a night spent in his truck. His neck and back ached, his knees cracked, and the view of the closed and locked motel room door made him regret so many words and actions.

He stood next to Zane by the vehicle, waiting for Sierra to exit. What had he been thinking, giving into temptation? At least Sierra had been wise enough to push him away. He couldn't be angry at her, but he could wish he'd never caused her pain, that he'd never given in to his own feelings.

He would never stop wanting her, but he couldn't risk her, not for his own desires. Not when danger stalked him every hour of every day. Not when his past had proved how deadly his chosen career was, not just to himself, but to those he cared about.

The motel room opened, and Sierra stepped into the light. She'd chosen another long, flowing dress that clung to her fake belly. The cornflower blue brought out a sparkle in her eyes, and the red of her wig made her skin appear like alabaster.

She was beautiful. She closed the door behind her, avoiding his gaze. The shadows beneath her eyes made him wince with guilt.

"What the hell happened between the two of

you?" Zane asked in a low breath. "She's frozen you into the arctic."

"Not her fault, Zane. It's mine. All mine."

Before Zane could respond, Sierra joined them. She shifted her bag on her shoulder. "I ran the wives' names this morning and discovered something *very* interesting in my background check. Diane Manley."

"Travis Manley's wife?" Rafe asked, reaching for her bag.

She ignored his outstretched hand and opened the passenger door of the truck, slipping her purse onto the floorboards. "Diane's father remarried when she was a teenager. The woman's last name was Leighton."

"As in Curtis Leighton?" Rafe asked, feeling the click of a few pieces falling into place.

"Your drug dealer," Sierra confirmed. "The rest of the wives and families checked out pretty clean. A few bankruptcies and brushes with the law, but nothing serious. Certainly nothing to imply they'd have anything to do with laundering twenty-five million dollars."

Zane patted Sierra on the back. "Good job, sugar. You did better than I did. I kept running down never-ending trails on my search into John Beckel. The guy smells bad. I just don't know why."

"Keep looking, and follow up on Sierra's information," Rafe said. He glanced at his watch. "We'd better get moving."

"See you over there," Zane said. "I'll keep in touch."

He waved as he pulled out of the parking lot.

Rafe faced Sierra. "Search Diane's things if you can. Maybe we'll get lucky."

"I know what to do." Sierra slid into the truck and waited for him, staring out of the side window.

Boy, this was going to be fun. Trouble was, Rafe didn't blame her one bit. He sat behind the steering wheel and buckled his seat belt, but didn't start the truck.

Finally he let out a long sigh. "We have a job to do, and we have to work together. If I could bow out, I would, but—"

"We've established our cover. I know." Sierra slipped her Glock from her bag and placed it in the side pocket. "I'm fine, Rafe. Mallory and Chloe are all that matter. They are all that's between us."

"You're still my wife," he said with a frown. "Can you act like one?"

She gave him a false smile. "I can pretend as well as you do. In fact I've learned to fake it from the best. Now let's get to the rodeo."

His conscience stinging, Rafe yanked the

truck into gear. He trusted Sierra to do her part because she wanted Mallory and Chloe back. But he had destroyed their relationship, and the camaraderie and friendship they'd found over the last day.

Perhaps it was for the best, but the hole in his heart had tripled in size.

BY THE TIME they arrived at the rodeo, Sierra could barely stay still. She didn't know how much longer she could sit next to Rafe without letting her emotions take over. She couldn't figure out why her feelings were so volatile. Maybe her injury, maybe her terror for Mallory and Chloe, but it seemed as if she had no reserves, no control over her emotions.

Rafe held her hand lightly as they walked through the rear entrance of the arena. He turned her to him and lightly brushed his lips across hers. She closed her eyes and hated her heart for doing that pitter-patter of a response.

"Be careful," he said. "You find anything, you call me. No need to do this alone."

Except there was every need. She nodded and turned her back on him, heading toward the VIP section. She forced herself not to turn around. What else could be said?

She strode past a large concrete pillar. A

hand curled around her arm and whirled her around.

Her eyes widened at the man who gripped her tight. Mallory's ex, Bud Harrigan.

"I *knew* it was you, Sierra Bradford," he shouted, gripping her shoulders with both hands. He shook her. "I'd recognize those interfering blue eyes anywhere. What have you done with my wife and daughter?"

Shocked, Sierra froze, but only for a moment. She let her training take over and thrust her hands between his and directly at his nose. In a quick defensive move, she extricated herself from his hold.

Bud lost his balance and fell backward, hitting his head on the pillar. His eyes narrowed. Nose bloody and face flamed red, he jumped to his feet and lunged at her.

She sidestepped him. "I didn't do anything to Mallory or Chloe. But I think you did, Bud. Where are they?"

"Just like a woman. Trying to turn the truth on its head. I know you. Think new hair and getting yourself pregnant changes you?" He raked his gaze down her rounded body in disgust. "I knew you weren't as perfect as my wife believed."

With a move quicker than she'd expected,

he grabbed her arm and twisted it behind her. "Where is my wife?"

A loud shout erupted from the side. Sierra's arm wrenched back so hard she thought it might break, then suddenly she was free.

With one punch Rafe knocked Bud to the ground. Lifting him by the collar, Rafe shoved the man against a door. "You touch my wife again, and you won't live to see tomorrow."

Rafe's grip tightened; Bud's face grew purple.

Sierra tugged on Rafe's arm. "Let him go," she whispered. "You'll kill him."

"He deserves it. He touched you."

"Rafe." Zane's voice intruded. "You're attracting unwanted attention."

With a growl, Rafe eased his grip. Bud choked out a cough and wheezed in a couple of breaths.

Relieved Zane had stopped Rafe from killing Bud, Sierra glanced around. "We can't stay here."

"This way." Zane led them down a deserted hallway to the rodeo's main office. "Inside," he hissed. "You're just lucky the boss left for a meeting with his brother."

Rafe shoved Bud inside. Sierra followed.

"Who are you?" Bud panted, clutching at

Rafe's grip. "Where's my wife and kid? I know she knows."

With a disgusted grunt, Rafe released his grip, and Bud crumbled to the office floor. Rafe knelt next to him.

"Call Detective Foster," Rafe ordered Zane with a smile that didn't reach his eye. "He can sort out the situation. We'll let the cops search Bud here and see what they find."

Mallory's ex went pale, and he clutched his jacket pocket. "No, no, we don't have to call the cops. We can work this out. I can pay you. Just don't get the police involved."

"Sit down, Bud." Rafe pushed him back into a chair. "You're going to answer a few questions. And then maybe, just maybe, we won't call the cops."

Okay, Sierra knew Rafe's statement was a lie. No way would he let Bud go.

She stared down at Mallory's ex. "When did you last see Mallory and Chloe?"

Bud scowled. "Two weeks ago. I confronted her after I was served the new custody agreement. Chloe is *my* kid. I have every right to see her. It's *your* fault she's ignoring my phone calls. Your fault she divorced me, you meddling bitch." He rose from the chair and charged at Sierra.

Rafe grabbed his collar, slamming him back

into his seat. "You try that again, *Bud*, and I'll give you a demonstration on how Uncle Sam taught me to interrogate prisoners. You got it?"

Bud's eyes widened, and he stared at Rafe's patch. A loud gulp escaped him.

Zane stood over Bud and stretched out his hand. "Give me your phone."

Bud spit in his face.

Rafe stepped forward, looming over Bud with a scowl Sierra wouldn't want directed at her. Ever.

"Let's try this again." Zane wiped his cheek and pinned Bud with a harsh glare. "Hand over your phone, or we call the cops and you explain the plastic baggie full of pills in your pocket."

With a curse, Bud yanked his phone from his pocket and shoved it at Zane.

The computer expert tapped the screen for a few minutes. "He's telling the truth. He's been trying to call Mallory for the past four days. He didn't do it."

Sierra's knees buckled, and she clutched at the door frame.

Rafe propped her up.

"What the hell is going on here?" Bud shouted. "What are you talking about?"

"Who sold you the pills?"

"I'm not saying anything else," Bud said. "Not without a lawyer."

"That can be arranged," Rafe said with a smile. "That can be arranged."

Chapter Ten

Sierra stood at the base of the steps leading into the arena. She wrapped her arms around her body and shivered. Rafe stood by her side. The last several minutes had shifted their relationship yet again, but she doubted it would ever be the same on a personal level. However, they could find a way to work together. She believed that now.

"Bud may not know what happened to Mallory and Chloe, but he could still give away my identity if he talks to the wrong person," she said, clutching her bag, taking comfort in the Glock's presence.

"Cade confiscated the drugs on Bud, enough to suggest an intent to distribute. His blood alcohol level was twice the legal limit. It'll take him some time to sober up before they can interview him," Rafe said. "Cade will continue questioning him and let us know of any leads.

Ransom's going to run interference with an attorney, but in reality, we only have until tomorrow morning to figure this out. After that, we'll have to face the cops and explain everything."

"So we have today to find Mallory and Chloe." Her gut roiled, and it had nothing to do with the smell of fresh horse manure. "The money has to come from the sale of drugs. What else is there?"

Several spectators jostled past them. Rafe placed his body between hers and the crowd.

"I agree," he said. "I'll work the brother, and—"

"I'll focus on Diane and see where that leads."

A bevy of announcements started droning from the arena.

"I'd better get you seated," he said. He frowned. "She may not be involved at all. With her brother dealing, she could simply be an innocent bystander."

"I hope so." Sierra straightened her dress. "I like her. But she sees things. I get the impression she's very sharp. She watches people. She knows where the secrets are buried. If she's not guilty, she may be able to provide us with another lead."

Rafe touched her back, and they made their way through the arena. "Zane's going to keep digging into the records. He thought he'd found some hidden files yesterday. He's going to attempt to decrypt them."

Sierra breathed in deeply. "I've been adding up the numbers in my head, Rafe. Five million dollars a year is a lot of oxycodone."

"You caught onto that, too." Rafe stroked his jaw. "We're missing something. Just keep your eyes and ears open for anything that doesn't quite fit. You'll know it when you see it. You've got good instincts."

Sierra pasted on a smile as she made her way to the VIP section of the arena. "Showtime," she whispered.

"Well, if it isn't our newest member," Nancy cooed. "You're looking mighty glowy today, Sarah."

Sierra touched her belly. "She's being active today."

"I know that feeling," Diane said, jostling her sobbing baby before slipping a bottle into the boy's mouth. He settled in her arms and sucked down the milk.

"He eats like a champ," Rafe commented.

Diane smiled. "Gets that from his daddy."

Rafe pulled Sierra into his arms. "See you later, honey. Wish me luck."

She closed her eyes and let him kiss her, trying to remind herself his embrace was just part of the job, that it didn't mean anything. But the gentleness of his lips broke her heart.

"Fan yourself, ladies," Nancy said.

Rafe's cheeks reddened at the brazen compliment. "I think I'd better get out of the line of fire." He tipped his Stetson. "Ladies."

The entire group watched Rafe walk away. "That man could be the centerfold for this year's rodeo cowboy calendar." Nancy sent Sierra a narrowed gaze. "You think he'd take his clothes off for charity?"

She nearly choked. "Umm… I don't think so."

"Don't tell me he's shy."

"No, but he's private." And Sierra realized how true her statement was. Rafe had revealed more to her the last few days about his past than he'd told anyone. Certainly Noah had shared what an enigma CTC found Rafe. How he'd seemed to have sprung full grown when he'd arrived at basic training—without a history, without connections. It was one of the main reasons Noah had warned her off the operative.

Sierra sat in front of Diane and twisted in her seat. "Rafe's pretty sore today," she offered. "How's Travis?"

Diane's expression dropped. "Hurting. More than he'll let on. He needs to manage the pain in his neck, but he refuses. Can't afford the doctor visits and meds. So he toughs it out."

"Rafe refused to see the doc yesterday, and he was up all night hurting. I don't know what to do," Sierra said with a sigh—at least some of her statement bore a resemblance to the truth.

Nancy clicked her tongue. "There are ways to get what he needs even if you're short on funds. *If* you're willing to take a chance."

Sierra blinked and shifted from facing Diane to Nancy. "I'm willing to do whatever it takes."

"See how it goes today," Nancy said with a pat. "I might have a solution for you."

Had Nancy just become their prime suspect?

"How's the nausea today, Sarah?" Diane asked, shifting the conversation. "I was lucky. Mine only lasted the first fourteen weeks or so."

"I threw up every morning until that baby came out," Nancy groaned. "And my breasts, my gosh, I don't know who started the rumor that women get all sexually hot and bothered during their pregnancy. Mine just hurt like the dickens."

Several women nodded in agreement. One, though, turned bright red.

Sierra stilled in her seat. Surreptitiously she touched the side of her left breast, where Archimedes had left his mark, then her right. Only now did she realize they'd both been feeling strangely tender for a couple of weeks. She'd blamed it on the scar.

Quickly she did a calculation. Her last period had been before Archimedes had kidnapped her.

Then there was the other important fact. A night of passion. Two months ago. With Rafe. In a motel. And the first time. No condom.

Oh my God.

"Sarah, you're looking a little green."

Nausea.

It couldn't be.

She swallowed deeply, her mind whirling at the possibility. She touched her belly. This couldn't be happening.

"Ladies and gentlemen, our bull riders have just drawn for their rides. First up, Travis Manley will be riding Evil Genius." The announcer went through several other assignments. Sierra's nails bit into her palms as each name was read. "Rafe Vargas…oh boy, folks. Rafe drew Angel Maker. Send a prayer up for our newest cowboy."

Sierra swayed in her seat.

Nancy propped her up and fanned her with her program. "Don't you worry, gal. It'll be okay. Those bullfighters will take care of your man."

"Turn your attention to the south chute, folks.

Travis Manley is currently ranked second over-all. He was scoreless in round one. Let's see if he can go over the top in the second round."

Sierra blinked and tried to focus on the chute. Travis nodded. The silver-gray bull roared into the arena. She forced herself to observe Diane. The woman's mouth had tightened into a thin line. Sierra had no idea if Diane was up to any-thing criminal, but she was obviously worried about her husband.

The buzzer sounded. The crowd roared. Eight seconds.

Travis should jump off the bull.

He didn't.

A loud gasp washed through the crowd.

"Help him out, fellows!" the announcer yelled.

"His hand's stuck," Nancy whispered, her own face paling.

Travis's body flailed on top of the huge animal. The bull slammed onto its side, and Travis's leg was caught beneath the beast.

A gasp went through the crowd. Diane shot to her feet. "Travis!"

The bull vaulted to its feet, but Travis lay still in the dirt. Two bullfighters herded the bull into the chute, then they motioned wildly for a stretcher.

"I have to go to him," Diane muttered.

"I'll take the baby." Nancy scooped up the boy. "You go."

One of the other women hooked her arm with Diane's to accompany her. She left as if in a daze.

The entire VIP area had gone solemn and silent. Sierra met Nancy's gaze. "Will he be okay?"

Nancy frowned. "All depends on where that bull stomped on him, but he wasn't moving, and that's never good."

Sierra's entire body had chilled. Rafe had to ride Angel Maker. She'd known bull riding was one of the most dangerous sports in the country, but she hadn't realized. Not really.

Rafe could die.

She touched her belly. She had so much to say to him. If she was right, everything between them had changed.

"Hey, little guy, you need to burp?" Nancy asked Diane's baby. "Sarah, could you get me a cloth out of his diaper bag?"

Sierra tugged the multipocketed satchel to her. She opened one compartment and saw only diapers.

"Try the front," one of the women said. "I think that's where she keeps her burp cloths."

Sierra dug into another cubby and handed

the cloth to Nancy. She paused for a moment, feeling strange rifling through someone else's things. Stiffening her back, she dug into the main compartment. "Do you need a diaper, too?" she asked, to cover her search.

Her hand encountered several plastic bags in one of the main pockets. Heart pounding, Sierra pulled out a disposable diaper and stilled. Beneath a layer of diapers were what might be fifty or more bags of pills.

Bud wasn't the drug supplier. Neither was Nancy. Diane Manley was.

THE COWBOYS BEHIND the chute had gone solemn. Travis Manley hadn't regained consciousness yet. Rafe didn't have much time left before his ride. He slipped away from the noise and preparations, and dialed a number.

"King." Jared's voice snapped out a greeting.

"What do you know about Angel Maker?" Rafe asked his friend.

"You drew that spawn of the devil." Jared let out a low whistle. "Great bloodlines. No cowboy's ever lasted eight seconds. In fact, I considered adding his gene pool to my stock, but even I don't know if I'm willing to pay the going rate for his genetic material." He chuckled. "Then again, I probably will."

"That's not what I'm asking."

"I know. Look, the thing that gets the riders is they psych themselves out from the start. They believe he's unpredictable, but he isn't. If he leaves the chute toward his left, he'll kick that way a few times and then do a major spin to the right. Most bulls have a preference. Angel Maker's ambidextrous. If he leaves the shut toward his right, he'll end up spinning left. That's when most of his riders lose their balance. Five or six seconds in.

"If you can stay centered during that the first spin, you've got a fighting chance."

Rafe rubbed the sore spot at the back of his neck. He might just survive this ride after all.

"Thanks, J.K. I owe you one."

Adjusting his patch, Rafe strode into the staging area. "You ready to face the demon, Vargas?" Kurt Prentiss asked.

"As ready as I'll ever be."

"We've got an extra bullfighter for Angel Maker. We'll get you out," the cowboy said.

"Vargas," the stager announced. "You're up."

Rafe climbed up to the top of the chute and stared down at the black devil known as Angel Maker. The bull snorted, his hooves dancing. He was the biggest bull Rafe had ever seen. He let out a long, slow breath and checked the strap. No tampering. He met Kurt's gaze. The cowboy nodded.

"Just you and me, Angel Maker," Rafe muttered.

He adjusted his grip on the rope and lowered himself on top of the bull. The moment his weight hit the beast's back he nodded.

The chute opened.

Angel Maker took off to the right.

Time slowed. Rafe fought against his instincts and leaned right.

Sure enough Angel Maker spun left, and Rafe's posture gave him just enough balance not to fly off the back of the animal.

Rafe knew the crowd screamed, but all he could hear was his blood rushing in his head and a slow count.

One. Two. Three. Four. Five. Six. Seven. Eight.

The siren sounded.

Rafe released the rope and jumped clear of the bull. The damned thing rushed him, head down. Rafe raced to the gate and vaulted up and over.

A roar sounded through the crowd. Rafe's gaze immediately went to the VIP stands.

Sierra had vanished.

IN THE STANDS, the crowd's roar washed over Sierra. She pressed her head lower between her knees.

Every last spectator in the arena stood cheering. "Rafe. Rafe. Rafe."

The chant didn't stop. He'd done the impossible.

Nancy bent down and rubbed her back. "Your man's looking for you," she said. "I think he's worried."

Sierra closed her eyes and sucked in a deep breath. She stood, struggling not to sway, and immediately Rafe's gaze pinned her in place.

The clamoring and boot stomping, the applause and shouts faded to nothing. Only the two of them existed for that moment. She'd always thought those fade-away shots in the movies were a trick of the director, but it was real.

As if she were in a trance, Sierra made her way down to the bottom row of seats. Rafe climbed back into the arena and raced across the dirt. He vaulted over a fence and then up to the bleachers. He wrapped his arms around her and buried his head in her shoulder.

"Told you it was like riding a bike," he whispered in her ear.

"Liar." She held him close, unable to speak around the fear still caught in her throat. "Don't do that again," she said. "I can't take it."

She placed her hand over her belly. *And neither can our baby.*

Chapter Eleven

With cheering crowds surrounding them, Sierra clung to Rafe as if her life depended on it. In many ways it did. She just wished she knew what the future would hold. How would he react to her unexpected news?

She touched his dusty face. "We need to talk."

"You got a lead?"

Rafe had just faced death, and he'd shoved it aside a lot faster than she could have. Her body stilled. How could she have forgotten the reason they were here together? Even for a moment. Telling him the news would have to wait. She relayed what she'd discovered about Diane and the drugs in her diaper bag. Then about Nancy's strange offer.

"I wish I could say I'm surprised, but not a whole lot shocks me anymore. They could be working it together. Travis, too."

"I hope he's not in on it," Sierra said. "For their son's sake."

Rafe pulled out his phone. "I'll text Zane. He can do a deep dive into her finances." Once he'd sent the message, he pocketed the device and took her hands in his. "You really came through."

"Then why does it leave such a bad taste in my mouth?" Sierra frowned. "Undercover feels like a betrayal."

With one eye on the VIP wives, he raised her hand to his lips. "Sometimes it's hard to tell which relationships are real, and which aren't."

He turned her palm face up and caressed it with his thumb. A tingle centered in Sierra's belly. Her feelings were real, but was this all an act? How could she tell?

He slipped his hand into hers. "Let's find Mallory and Chloe."

They climbed the bleachers. When they reached the reserved section, Rafe tipped his hat once again and gifted them with a smile. "Ladies."

"You showed Angel Maker what-for, Rafe." Nancy chortled. "Congratulations."

"Thank you. I got lucky that time."

"I doubt luck had anything to do with it. I think you're just that good."

Sierra leaned over Nancy and forced her

voice into a low whisper. "You said you had a suggestion for Rafe's pain? He's putting on a good front, but I can tell he's hurting, and it'll be worse tomorrow."

"Couldn't tell it by me. He must be an expert at hiding what he doesn't want known. However, I do have a solution for you." Nancy grinned and pulled out a card. "Acupuncture. Kept my man riding all these years. The doc is my son. He'll give you a discount if Rafe's willing to become a human pincushion."

Sierra's shoulders lightened with relief. She wanted to hug the woman in appreciation for not being a criminal. "Thanks, Nancy." She accepted the card. "I think we'll head over to medical. Rafe wants to check on Travis."

She made a point of thanking the women for their support and advice to distract them while Rafe grabbed the diaper bag. He climbed down a few steps, and she quickly extricated herself and followed.

When she reached his side, Sierra glanced over her shoulder. "Eventually they'll miss the baby's supplies."

"It doesn't matter. We need to talk to Diane. See what she knows and find out who's working with her, because she didn't pull off this abduction by herself."

They wove through the stands and made

their way to the on-site medical clinic. Zane was waiting for them, and the frown on his face gave Sierra a chill.

They veered toward him. "What's wrong?" Rafe asked.

"I don't think she's the key to finding Mallory and Chloe."

He handed Sierra a printout. "I found a separate account under Diane's maiden name, which is why we missed it. She and her brother are clearly in this together, but look at the totals. Five years' worth of drug dealing, and it's nowhere near twenty-five million. In fact, they're barely making a profit. She's not our target."

"Are you saying she wasn't involved in the abduction?" The grim possibility that they'd been searching in the wrong direction sent her pulse racing in panic. Had they wasted the most critical time to find Mallory and Chloe assuming the wrong motive for the kidnapping? Had their entire investigation been a colossal mistake? "Then who else could it be?" Sierra stalked over to Diane. Zane tried to stop her, but she avoided his grasp.

The woman stood fearfully watching the paramedics stabilizing Travis and immobilizing his leg. Sierra clasped Diane's arm. "I need to talk to you. Right now."

Diane shook Sierra off. "What are you doing? Can't you see my husband's hurt? Leave me alone."

Rafe sidled up to Sierra and raised the diaper bag. "We need to discuss your little side business, Mrs. Manley."

Her brother rushed out of the shadows and tried to grab the bag. "Leave her alone."

"Back off, Spider," Rafe said, keeping a tight hold on the evidence. "Don't make it worse. Because you're both going to jail. For a long time."

Diane cast a worried glance at Travis. She gnawed on her lip and led them away from the entrance. "You don't understand. Can't you just forget what you saw? I'm not hurting anyone."

"You're dealing drugs." Sierra crossed her arms over her chest.

"I'm selling pain relief to men who can't afford to get what they need. I don't make any money." Diane lifted her chin. "I'm doing what has to be done so we can survive."

At the intense defense, Sierra paused. "Explain it to me."

"Most of the cowboys here can't afford insurance or prescriptions," Diane said. "Rodeo is hard on the body. Some of these guys can't go from event to event and finish in the money without some help. Especially as they get older. No money means no food on the table."

"Does your husband know?" Rafe asked.

The horrified expression on Diane's face made the truth clear. Travis had no knowledge of what his wife had done.

A wave of disappointment smothered Sierra's hope. She rubbed her temples as her mind tried to process the latest setback. "You didn't kidnap Mallory Harrigan and her daughter, did you?"

"The secretary? Why would anyone do such a thing?"

Diane couldn't have faked the shock or confusion. Sierra looked over at Rafe, who shook his head. "We're at a dead end."

RAFE PLACED A hand on Travis Manley's shoulder. The cowboy had cheated death one more time at the hands of a bull. He'd have some rehab ahead, but he'd walk again. Maybe even ride again.

His family would never be the same.

Travis held his son in his arms and watched as Detective Cade Foster Mirandized his wife and brother-in-law. Two cops led the pair away in handcuffs.

"I should've known," he muttered, patting the baby's back. "She gave me those pills, said the doc had given them to us for free. I wanted to believe her."

His son reached toward Diane. "Mama. Mama."

She turned to give them one last regretful look before disappearing around a corner, in custody.

Travis shifted his body, wincing, and lifted his gaze to Rafe. "You're not here to launch a comeback, are you? You were here to catch them."

"Sorry, Travis. Your wife ended up on our radar, but not because we were searching for a ring selling prescription drugs. I'm here to find a kidnapper."

"Diane would never kidnap..." His voice trailed off. "Of course, I didn't think it was possible she could be a drug dealer, either."

"We're pretty certain she's not involved in the abduction," Rafe said. "If it's any consolation, Diane didn't make any real money on the medication. Money was never her motive. She did it to help you and everyone here. She made just enough to cover expenses."

"The right reason doesn't make the act okay."

How well Rafe knew that. "The world can be gray sometimes. Believe me, I know more than most."

Travis didn't appear convinced. His skepticism reminded Rafe he'd asked himself more than once over the last few months if he'd lived too long in the murky space between black and white.

He might not be able to help Travis accept his wife's choice, but he could assist with a better outcome. "Look, Travis, I can hook you up with a good lawyer who won't charge you too much."

"I hadn't even thought that far." After a brief hesitation, Travis nodded. "I guess I'm a little… stunned right now. Not thinking too clearly, and I don't believe that's because a bull kicked me until he knocked me out. Thank you. I owe you one."

Rafe went silent for a moment. They needed a break, and his gut told him this bull rider was worth the risk of revealing the truth. "Travis, you might be able to help me right now. You've been with the circuit awhile. You know the players. We discovered twenty-five million dollars has been laundered through the rodeo in the last five years. Any idea who or what might be involved with that kind of money? Any rumors of guns, drugs, people being bought and sold?"

Travis stroked his son's cheek, and Rafe recognized a light of recognition filtering into the man's eyes.

"I've got a pretty good idea," Travis murmured under his breath. "Talk to Harlen Anderson. Diane mentioned the other day the guy wore a thousand-dollar pair of shoes mucking around in the stalls. Who does that if they're not rolling in dough?"

The nondescript almost forgettable veterinarian. Interesting. He could pretty much come and go as he pleased. He'd have reason to go practically anywhere at the rodeo. That much freedom would make a good cover for a whole lot of trouble.

Rafe shook Travis's hand. "Thanks. Get better. And once again, I'm sorry."

"You didn't make the choice," Travis said with a frown. "She did."

Another family destroyed. Rafe had lost count how many times he'd been directly involved in this kind of devastation. Sometimes it was deserved. Sometimes, like today, a good man was an unwitting victim who would have to raise his son alone. At least for the foreseeable future.

If nothing else, he could inform Sierra of some not-bad news. Since they'd interviewed Diane, Rafe knew they both had begun to wonder if Mallory and Chloe Harrigan would ever be found. Especially since no ransom note had been delivered.

He left the medical clinic and joined Sierra and Zane across the corridor. "I may have a potential lead."

Sierra's eyes lit up before Rafe could finish his thought.

"It's not solid enough to go full force. We have to review every note, every statement, every search. If something gives you a niggle, set it aside."

"I've pulled everything off the rodeo books I can," Zane said. "With your cover blown, I might be better off spending time in front of the keyboard instead of continuing on."

"If you're certain you have copies of all the files you need," Rafe said, when a familiar figure caught his eye. He nodded Detective Foster over.

Cade shook Rafe's hand. "Not bad work for a couple of spies."

"We didn't exactly arrest a major drug lord," Rafe countered. "And we're light on leads to find Mallory and Chloe."

"That's why I stopped by," Cade said. "I don't know if it helps, but someone in the department ran your name through the system earlier today. They also searched for information on a woman named Sierra Bradford yesterday. *Not* Sarah Vargas."

Rafe let out a long, slow breath. Whoever

the puppet master was on this operation still had strings in the police department, and in the rodeo. His lips thinned and he met Sierra's gaze, knowing she understood the potential implications.

"They might know my true identity," she said.

"But *who* knows?" Rafe faced Cade. "Who ran the searches? Do they *really* know Sierra and Sarah is the same person, or is it guesswork?"

"Sarah Vargas wasn't searched, so maybe not. As to the identity of the perp, the system indicated that a cop on traffic patrol ran the search. No way he could have worked the computer and ticketed a speeding car at the same time."

"If they ran my name yesterday, I think they traced my weapon," Sierra said. "I didn't reveal my name during the abduction, but they have my gun. It's traceable."

"Makes sense," Cade said, working the rim of his hat. "But why would the same cop run Rafe's name today?"

"They know," Rafe said. "They have to."

Which meant they no longer had the element of surprise, and Mallory and Chloe's chances of survival just plummeted. From Sierra's alarmed expression, she had already come to the same conclusion.

He sidled up to her and rubbed her back in slow, circular motions, hoping to reassure her, or at least offer the only comfort he could.

"Get out of my way," a furious voice shouted.

Rafe whirled toward the ruckus, and he placed himself between Sierra and the disturbance, hand pausing near his weapon.

An irate John Beckel rushed into the corridor, his face red and sweaty. "What the hell is going on here? I've just tried to convince dozens of scared families that this rodeo isn't too dangerous to attend. They're walking out. I'm losing thousands of dollars every minute."

He shoved Cade backward. "I had an agreement with the cops. You broke it."

"Really, Mr. Beckel. And what arrangement might that be? For us to ignore a drug operation in your facility?"

Beckel huffed and tugged out his phone. "I'm calling your captain, Detective… Foster, is it? He'll bust you down to patrol so quick, you won't have a career left."

Before Beckel could place the call, his attention snapped to Zane. "And what are *you* doing here?" His cheeks went blotchy. "You know what. I don't like you, I don't like your tattoo. You're too big to be an accountant. You're fired!"

On a roll, Beckel pointed at Rafe. "And you. I knew you were trouble. I don't care if you did ride Angel Maker and the whole world wants to interview you. You're no longer welcome here. I'm banning you from competition and from my rodeo."

He whirled on Sierra. "And you…" He glanced down at her belly. "I don't know *what* to tell you, but I'd get away from all of them."

Cade stepped forward and faced the irate man. "You need to calm down, sir, before you say something you'll regret."

"Get them off my property," Beckel blustered. "All of them."

"Not until we get some answers," Rafe said, his jaw tightening. Seemed like the good ol' boy John Beckel pretended to be was just an illusion.

"I don't have to speak to any of you." He started to stalk off, but Cade stopped him with a firm hand. "Mr. Beckel, I strongly suggest you reconsider. I know you'd prefer to answer questions privately instead of in front of a lot of people with cell phones. And cameras."

Beckel tapped his phone and put it to his ear. "Warren, I need our lawyer at the rodeo. Call him now."

At the mention of legal counsel, Rafe knew Cade would have to back off, but not everyone had to follow the rules. He stepped in front of Cade until he stood boots-to-boots with John Beckel. "I only have two questions. What are your dealings with Harlen Anderson, and what did you do with Mallory and Chloe Harrigan?"

FOR SOME REASON Sierra had hoped they'd return to their motel room in triumph—or maybe even having found Mallory and Chloe. Instead, she sat with Rafe in his truck, her body limp with disappointment, her heart numb with fear.

Their accomplishment today—they'd ruined several lives. The drug operation had been Diane's choice, but Travis's shocking sadness and his son's inconsolable sobs had broken her heart.

As for Mallory and Chloe, Beckel either had the talent of an Oscar-winning actor or was innocent. Sierra didn't even want to put her doubts into words. They may already be too late to save them. Just the thought made her eyes burn with despair.

"I really believed Diane or her brother or even Bud would lead us to Mallory, Rafe. What are we going to do?"

"We regroup and start from scratch," Rafe

said, his tone biting and frustrated. "Figure out what we missed."

Sierra didn't take it personally. Rafe didn't like to lose, and she took comfort in the determined line of his jaw. He hadn't given up, but she couldn't deny her gut twisted with uncertainty.

He squeezed her hand. "Zane's meeting us back at the motel. Maybe he's been able to break that encrypted file from Beckel's office."

"I thought he might be guilty, but he's all show."

"And little substance," Rafe said. "I doubt he could pull this off. He might get lucky a time or two, but not for five years straight. He certainly was cagey about Harlen, though. Didn't want to give us any information."

"Do you think Harlen's involved?" Sierra asked.

"The search of his clinic at the rodeo didn't turn up anything. Ransom's checking him out. Hopefully we'll hear from the boss soon."

Which meant the only thing left to do would be wait, and search their records to find Mallory and Chloe.

Sierra clutched her purse tight, trying to center the whirlpool that had become her life. If she were honest, ever since Archimedes had taken her, nothing had been the same—and if she was right, her life had changed forever.

She just prayed Mallory and Chloe would be a part of it.

"You look pale again, honey. Are you sure it's allergies and you're not getting sick?"

Then there was the lie she'd told Rafe. That she'd needed some allergy medication from the pharmacy. Instead, she'd picked up two pregnancy kits.

She grimaced at the falsehood, but nodded. If she was wrong—and she probably was given all the stress over the last few months—she didn't want to worry Rafe.

No, that wasn't true. In reality she didn't want to face his reaction at all, because she had no idea how he would respond and, in a corner of her heart, a small hope for a future with him still burned too brightly.

He rounded the truck and helped her out of the vehicle as if she were spun of glass. If she were pregnant, she'd have to break him of the hovering, or she'd kill him before their baby arrived.

And there she went again, assuming the best. When a deep foreboding had settled at the base of her neck.

Her heart longed for a happy ending that her head recognized to be unlikely.

She glanced down at her disguise. "I'm stripping out of this outfit," she said. "My entire body aches. I'll be thrilled to say goodbye to Sarah Vargas once and for all. What a nightmare."

At her words her gaze snapped to Rafe. She hadn't meant that the way it sounded.

Rafe had stilled, frozen midmovement. His frown had deepened, but he gave her a stiff nod, opening the motel room door. "I guess we're getting an annulment."

Before she could apologize, Princess Buttercup bypassed her and streaked to Rafe, jumping into his arms.

"What's wrong, P.B.?" he asked, stroking the cat with a reassuring hand. "You're trembling."

Sierra's heart melted at the big bad spy guy cuddling the trembling cat. She never would have guessed he could be that gentle. If he chose, Rafe would make a wonderful, loving father. She was certain of that. She just didn't know if he'd want that life.

Lifting her suitcase, she set it on the bed to retrieve a change of clothes. She gripped the zipper tag and yanked it open. She'd have her answer in a few minutes. Her gut ached with tension.

A rattling sounded from the suitcase.

Sierra froze. "What the…?"

Like a scene from a horror movie, a small snake slithered from between the zipper's silver teeth. The creature hissed. The rattle at the end of the tail shook in warning.

She couldn't breathe. The snake's body coiled, its triangular-shaped head rose. Rafe dropped the cat, raced across the room and swept her back just as the snake struck. It missed her by inches. Then, to her horror, at least two dozen small rattlers poured from the bag.

"They're more dangerous than the large ones," Rafe whispered in her ear. "Concentrated venom."

They poured in a slithering mass to the floor. Rafe pulled her toward the door. "Come on!"

At their side, Princess Buttercup hissed and pounced toward the rattlers.

"No!" Sierra shouted.

"Stop, P.B." Rafe reached for the animal.

The angry feline scooted out of the way and bounded toward the snakes. A rattling symphony erupted. Princess Buttercup's back went up, but within seconds, she slunk back.

Rafe scooped her into his arms, and they all quickly backed out of the motel room, slamming the door shut.

"Did they bite her?" Sierra asked, whirling.

Rafe palpated the cat's paws. "I don't think

so. She would've yelped. Snakebites hurt like hell. If she becomes at all lethargic or seems sick, we'll have to get her help quickly."

He scratched her ears. "You brave, crazy cat, what did you think you were doing?"

"Protecting us. She's an attack cat after all." Sierra shivered. "Those snakes weren't an accident."

"No, I'd call it attempted murder."

Rafe called Zane. "We're moving locations. They've obviously figured out Sarah is Sierra, and I'm not taking any chances. She's not going back to the rodeo. Too dangerous. Too many *accidents* could happen. She'll work the keyboards from now on."

Rafe ended the call and shot her a challenging glare. "I'm not arguing with you about this decision or your reassignment. I'd pull anyone off undercover once it's blown."

Sierra cradled her fake belly. "I'm not arguing."

"Okay, then." That had gone better than he'd hoped. Strangely well, in fact. He started the car and handed Sierra the cat. "She's trembling. She could use some TLC."

"Me, too. Who would do something like that, Rafe? It's a horrible way to die."

"A malicious way to kill. I have to wonder if our perp is irrational enough to believe that murder by a bunch of snakes would look like an accident."

She gasped. "Rafe, we can't just leave those snakes there. The maid or owner could walk in."

As she spoke, Rafe called the motel's owner to warn him. "He's contacting animal control, and I'll arrange for Zane to collect our things and rendezvous at the new location."

Sierra studied her fingers drifting through Princess Buttercup's paws. "Do you think this means Mallory and Chloe are alive?"

He didn't answer her, and her heart fell.

"I see. I'd hoped—"

"I wish I knew, Sierra. I really do. All I can tell you is we're getting too close to something someone doesn't want uncovered. Something they're willing to kill for."

RAFE THOUGHT OF himself as transient most of the time, but even for him, three motels in two days was excessive. "We've been tough on accommodations," he commented to Sierra, who'd finally ditched her disguise and was planning to plant herself in front of her laptop once it arrived.

While Rafe couldn't deny her figure evoked a passionate response, her more rounded look had stirred something primal within him.

In his mind, he could picture her pregnant and happy. He just couldn't see himself by her side. She'd be married to some banker or accountant, safe, protected.

Loved by another man.

His hand squeezed the plastic cup he held into shards. He dropped them into the trash can. Okay, so he was jealous. He'd have to get used to the idea of her future. And his. Alone.

A knock sounded at their door. Rafe peered through the peephole and opened the door.

Zane stood there, weighed down with their bags.

"Next time, carry your own luggage," he groused, dropping everything but her computer bag with attitude.

Sierra stood frozen, staring at her suitcase with suspicion.

"No snakes," she said. "I know that in my head, so why don't I want to open the bag?"

"Even Indiana Jones hates snakes," Rafe said.

She tried to smile at his lame attempt at a joke, but it didn't reach her eyes. Sierra watched him with that same fidgety gaze he'd become too accustomed to since he'd ridden Angel Maker.

He'd expected her to be jittery. Who wouldn't be after a slithering nightmare come to life, but

Sierra had faced much worse with Archimedes. This time, though, she displayed a caution he hadn't perceived before. Even then.

Rafe met Zane's concerned gaze. His co-worker recognized the change, too.

She ignored the bag on the floor and carried her computer bag to the table. She set it down and plugged it in, but didn't settle in the chair waiting for it to boot. Instead, she buzzed around the room like a hummingbird. She refused to light anywhere.

Because she didn't trust him to protect her? Then again, why would she? He couldn't blame her for that.

She passed by him for the fourth time, and he clasped her upper arm to stop her. "What's wrong?" he asked. "Why so nervous?"

Her gaze veered to the left. The universal avoidance pattern made him pause. What the hell was going on?

Zane cleared his throat. "While you two were playing with snakes, I came up with an interesting possibility."

"A lead?" Sierra leaned over his shoulder. "Are you sure?"

"Is anything about this case certain? It's a long shot, but right now it's all I've got." Zane opened his laptop. "Cade called me when he couldn't reach you."

Rafe glanced at his phone. Sure enough, he'd missed the call sometime around the snake attack. "What did he find out?"

"Cade broke Bud. He discovered two *very* interesting pieces of information. Bud bought his drugs from Diane Manley. Evidently he got hooked after a surgery five years ago."

"That explains a lot, but I don't see a connection to the kidnapping. We closed that loop," Sierra said with a frown. Her shoulders drooped.

"Perhaps not. But Bud's monthly income wasn't what I'd expected, either." Zane passed a printout to Sierra. "He makes too much. He finally admitted he works doing odd jobs at the rodeo. Not for John Beckel, for *Warren*."

Now that was a revelation. The invisible brother.

"The brains behind the money." Sierra's eyes sparked with interest as she scanned the document.

This was the Sierra Rafe knew and understood. He could see the wheels turning.

"On a hunch, I dug into him some more," Zane added. "He put up some barriers to my original searches with several layers of shell corporations, but I finally uncovered evidence that Warren Beckel isn't quite the angel he's painted himself to be. I found several fraud arrest records about twenty years ago. Charges were strangely dropped due to evidence tampering. My guess is he's been buying off law enforcement for a long time."

Zane shoved a file at Rafe, and he quickly scanned it. "Why didn't we see this before?"

"He's been perfecting hiding for two decades," Zane said. "I wouldn't have found it if Sierra hadn't shown me a few tricks on the Kazakhstan job a while back."

"Give me the endgame," Rafe said, handing Sierra the folder.

"Warren Beckel's fingers are knuckle-deep in a lot more pies than we thought. In addition to a slew of businesses, he owns quite a few properties. Including a parcel about a four-hour drive from here. He purchased it, but it's in John's name. Sitting empty in the middle of nowhere."

"That's strange," Sierra said.

"It gets better. The land is supposed to be deserted. However, when I pulled up recent satellite imagery—"

"And exactly how'd you access that?" Rafe asked his friend.

"Oh…" Zane hesitated. "I know a guy."

Which meant somehow he'd used his old contacts to grab Department of Defense images.

"I love you, Zane," Sierra said with feeling.

She kissed his cheek. The man's ears turned red, and Rafe scowled at her. He couldn't believe she'd said those words to Zane. Or that she'd kissed him.

And he certainly didn't like admitting how that small display of friendship needled at him.

"I'm relieved you're on our team and not on the bad guys' side," she added. "So, what did the photos show? Did you see Mallory and Chloe?"

Zane shook his head. "Not enough resolution, but a couple of buildings *have* been placed on the property without permits. One's a mobile home. Not something Warren would normally purchase. He's more of a five-star-hotel kind of guy."

"But it would be a good place for the Beckel brothers to hide someone or something they didn't want found. Especially given Warren's history," Rafe surmised. "I like your thinking, Zane."

"The link to them is tenuous at best, and it may not hold up in court given what I had to do to uncover the links, but it's the best lead I've got."

"We'll worry about court once Mallory and Chloe are safe," Rafe said, "but I can see in your face that's not all."

"We have a big problem," Zane said. "I can't

call the local cops there to check the place out. Too many potential leaks, and according to Cade, the drugs confiscated from Diane are an identical match to a stash of black market prescription drugs the cops confiscated last year. Someone on the police force is clearly involved."

"We have to search the land," Sierra said. "But four hours away makes it an all-day round trip."

"That's what planes are for," Rafe said. "Zane could reach the place in an hour or so."

Zane grinned. "Great minds. I also took the liberty of calling Ransom. He's sending Léon this way to back you up."

"Excellent." Rafe liked the move. Léon's identity was a closely guarded secret, but the former heir to the small European country of Bellevaux had trained as an operative. Now living a new life, Léon had a skill set that rivaled Rafe's. If he couldn't have Noah on his six, Léon would do very nicely.

"While you're heading to the Beckels' land, Sierra and I will rework the rest of our evidence. Maybe we'll see something else we missed as we focused on the drug theory."

Zane nodded. "It's a plan." He handed Sierra a thumb drive. "I dumped the files I copied from the rodeo on it. Hopefully you'll see something I didn't."

He didn't add they were scraping the bottom of the barrel. They all knew it, so he quickly left to meet the CTC plane.

"Sounds like a good lead," Rafe said, turning to Sierra, surprised she hadn't said more.

She'd gone deathly white.

Alarmed, Rafe hurried over to her.

"Excuse me," she muttered. She covered her mouth, shoved past him and raced into the bathroom, carrying the pharmacy bag with her.

Rafe knocked softly on the door. "Sierra?"

She didn't respond.

"Sierra." He raised his voice. "Are you okay?"

He pressed his ear to the door and heard the sound of running water. He banged harder. "Answer me or I'm coming in."

"Give me a minute," she said, her voice thick with emotion. "Please."

Something was very wrong. He didn't know exactly what, but she had to be okay. He needed her.

A few minutes later Sierra exited the bathroom.

"How are you feeling? Do you need a doctor?"

She shook her head slowly. "I'm fine. For now."

The pensive look on her face made him pause. "What's wrong?"

She looked up at him with fear-laced eyes, clutching a small box.

"I'm pregnant."

Chapter Twelve

The motel room went completely silent. Sierra didn't want to look at Rafe. She should have waited to tell him, but she hadn't been able to stop herself from taking the test.

And once she'd seen the indicator...

"How long have you known?" he asked quietly.

At the strange caution, even resentment in his tone, her gaze flew to his in confusion. She saw an expression of what she first took as distrust and disbelief, but then she recognized the truth. Hurt and disappointment laced his eyes.

She thrust the pregnancy test into his hand. "I was certain thirty seconds ago, but I've only suspected a couple of hours. All those wives and their talk of babies and advice about symptoms." She grasped his arm. "I didn't keep this a secret, Rafe. I wouldn't."

He rubbed his face with his free hand. "I know you wouldn't."

She let go of him and stepped back. She'd had more than a moment to consider what to think, and she was still in a state of shock. She shouldn't be wishing that he would smile at her, take her in his arms and twirl her around in celebration.

She glanced away from his still stunned look. "I shouldn't have said anything. Not yet. We can talk about it later. For now, we have a job to do."

Struggling against the nausea that threatened to boil over, she turned her back. She'd work the computer, focus on Mallory and Chloe. She could do that.

He clasped her shoulders and gently turned her to him. "Hell, no. You should *definitely* have told me. You should have told me the moment you..." His voice trailed off. "You tried to say something. After the ride."

She nodded.

He tilted her face up to his and placed his hand on her still-flat belly. "How do you feel?"

"Nauseous. Scared. Emotional." Her eyes welled. "I've been thinking about Mallory and her Chloe. I already love our baby with everything I am, Rafe. I don't know what I'd do if something happened to her. I'd do whatever I must to protect her."

She blinked hard. "Look at me. I'm a mess."

He caught a tear with his knuckle. "I'm right there with you. And Sierra, I'd kill for her. And you. Without hesitation."

His good eye flashed with an intensity she'd never seen. "You want this baby."

She placed her hand on top of his. "I didn't plan on this, but I want it. Even though I'm terrified."

Rafe took in a shuddering breath. "Does that mean you want your baby's father, too?"

Before she could answer, a vibrating phone shattered the fragile moment. "Blocked call," he said. "I have to—"

Sierra chewed the inside of her lip to attempt a modicum of control. "Take it."

He tapped the speakerphone. "Vargas."

"I hear you're looking for me."

Sierra recognized the drawl from their first day at the rodeo.

"Harlen?"

"I also heard from a reliable source that you're looking for some very specific information," the vet said. "I'm ready to talk. Everything's imploding, and the boss is getting paranoid. He's making mistakes. But I need some guarantees."

"I'll do everything I can," Rafe said.

"No deal. You have no authority. I talk to you, I end up in jail. I can give you the identity of the kidnapper. And I didn't have *anything* to do with taking that woman and her child."

Sierra grabbed the phone from Rafe's hand. "Then who did? Where are they?" Sierra shouted.

"Sarah Vargas. Or should I say, Sierra Bradford. You've made a lot of people very angry."

Rafe pried the phone away from her hand. She paced back and forth, longing to leap through the phone at the call's other end and strangle that man until he talked.

"Turn yourself in, Harlen," Rafe said. "If you help us find Mallory and Chloe Harrigan, it'll go a long way to bettering your situation."

Harlen let out a sharp laugh. "Not hardly. I talk, I'm dead. And with a significantly more painful death than a few rattlers."

Rafe let out a curse. "That was your sick idea?"

"I didn't say that," Harlen argued. "But with a unit captain and a couple of his flunkies from the local police on the take, no way am I going anywhere near a police station until they're arrested. You want information, meet me at my office at the rodeo. And come alone. I guarantee, I'll give you want you want."

THE PROTECTIVE GROVE of trees served them well. Mallory used the trunk to stand. She searched the ground for a cane.

"Button, can you bring me that stick beneath that big tree?"

Chloe nodded. Her daughter had become more and more subdued as the night went on. Her lips were parched. Mallory knew she had to find water for them in the next few hours, or they wouldn't survive.

Her daughter returned with the stick. Mallory tested her weight against the straight piece of wood.

Ever so gingerly she set her foot on the ground and inch by inch added some weight.

When the pain didn't make her cry out, a smidgen of hope welled within her.

"Can you walk?" Chloe asked.

"Maybe, Button." Mallory moved the stick forward and took a tentative step. A sharp pain ratcheted through her ankle, but it didn't send her to her knees. She could live with it.

"Let's go find some water."

Chloe nodded listlessly. "I'm thirsty."

Slowly they made their way through the dense thicket. When they passed a large boulder, a sense of déjà vu hit Mallory. A horrifying sense of foreboding settled in her belly.

They walked a bit more until they reached another thick copse of trees. Mallory moved a limb aside. When she did, she gasped. The bumper of a red vehicle appeared.

"Look, Mommy, a car." Chloe pulled at her mother's hand.

Mallory held her daughter back. "We have to be careful and quiet and still."

"They may have something to drink. Or breakfast," she whispered. "Please."

"Maybe."

"Maybe means no," Chloe said, pouting.

"Shh, Button. Please."

Even though Chloe gave her a mutinous nod, Mallory had to take the chance. Her movements as quiet as possible given her injury, Mallory limped toward the clearing. First a red truck came into view. If only the owner had left the keys inside.

Then an all-too-familiar shack loomed off to her right. Mallory gripped the staff.

The cop's shack.

Her entire body froze with terror. They'd gone in one big circle.

Now what?

The police officer with the soulless eyes slammed out of the trailer. "That woman and kid didn't just disappear. We're three days' walk from anything. They have to be out there somewhere." He cradled a rifle in his arm. "I just received orders from the boss. If you see them, kill them. Kill them both."

Chloe let out a shrill squeal.

The cop turned toward the woods. "Glen, did you hear something?"

"N-no, sir."

Mallory stepped backward and came up against a large wall of muscle.

A hand clamped over her mouth and Chloe's.

"Be quiet, or you're dead," a voice whispered in her ear.

She froze. Oh God. They were caught.

RAFE PRESSED HARDER on the accelerator and glanced at Sierra. A baby. He still couldn't quite process the information, and somehow he had to find a way to focus on his job.

If he'd believed for one moment he could convince her to return to Denver—or even head to Carder—he would. But he knew the odds. Nonexistent.

Even now she flipped through a folder of printouts, searching for anything they'd missed. Once they reached the rodeo, she'd pull out her laptop. No way were they risking leaving any evidence alone in their motel room.

P.B. snuggled up against his thigh. He grown used to the miniature hot water bottle rubbing against him. He couldn't leave the silly creature alone in the room. Not after the snake attack. The poor beast hadn't stopped trembling. He turned the vehicle onto the street housing the rodeo. "You have your weapon?" he asked Sierra.

She nodded.

"I wish you would have stayed—"

"Don't even go there, Rafe. You could need backup." She held up her hand. "Before you say it, I already agreed to stay in the truck unless you don't check in on time. I promise."

Rafe's vehicle screeched into the empty parking lot. Cade had informed them that the rodeo had closed down early and the building evacuated pending a full investigation. In fact, John and Warren Beckel had both disappeared. He parked the car near a barrier for easy access and defense.

"You'll keep on your guard?" he asked.

"Of course," she said. She touched his arm. "Be careful."

"Don't worry." He cupped her face. "I have two big reasons to come back safe and sound."

He exited the vehicle and hurried to the back of the arena. Most of the horse trailers and RVs had vanished. He entered the oddly quiet hallway and, with silent footsteps, entered the vet clinic.

Harlen Anderson was crouched across the room.

"Get down," he shouted.

A shot rang out, hitting the concrete next to Rafe's feet. He dived toward Harlen, and both men scrambled behind the vet's desk.

"What's going on?"

Harlen wiped his brow. "He found out I called you. I don't know how—"

A loud boom sounded. Harlen's eyes went wide. A stain of blood bloomed across his chest.

He sank to the floor, his breathing harsh.

Rafe ripped the man's shirt and reached out for a wad of bandages on a nearby steel cart, but all the equipment in this room wouldn't save Harlen. Rafe had seen this kind of devastating chest injury too often, but that didn't mean he wouldn't fight for the man's life.

He pressed bandages as tightly as he could. Harlen grabbed his wrists.

"Photos," he whispered. "Phone."

His eyes closed, his head fell to the side. He was dead.

Rafe crouched lower. A shot came from one side, then the other. At least two shooters. A single pair of boots clomped forward. Another moved to the side. They were closing in.

Rafe glanced around. There was no back exit.

They had him trapped. He grabbed his phone from his back pocket. The glass was crushed. Damn. He couldn't warn Sierra.

"Might as well give it up, Vargas," a voice shouted. "You aren't getting out of here alive."

THE INSIDE OF the truck had warmed up quite a bit beneath the cloudless San Antonio sky. Sierra checked her watch for the umpteenth time. Where was he? He should've checked in by now.

Princess Buttercup let out a soft meow. Sierra stroked the cat's fur. "You know something's wrong, too, don't you?"

The cat butted her hand.

Unable to stay in one spot, Sierra twisted in her seat and peered through the window. What if something had gone wrong?

Her phone vibrated in her pocket. She grabbed it. "Hello? Rafe?"

"He won't be answering. Not now. Not ever."

Sierra shook her head. No, Rafe was fine. This man was lying. He had to be.

"Listen carefully," a gravelly voice whispered. "Or you'll end up just like Rafe. With a bullet hole straight to the chest."

"Who is this?" Sierra gripped the butt of her Glock. Her eyes stung. She knew better than to trust an anonymous caller. Except Rafe hadn't contacted her, and he'd promised.

"Ms. Bradford, I understand you've been looking for something. Something you'd do almost anything for in order to get it back."

The blood in Sierra's veins chilled, but her heart thudded and her pulse pounded in her ears. After all this effort, was the kidnapper really coming to her?

"I have Mallory and Chloe Harrigan."

"Are they all right?" The words spilled from Sierra's lips. *Calm down.* Focus. Be smart.

What would Rafe do?

He'd keep them talking. He'd try to learn more. She slid her finger to view her messaging application. No text from him. Where was he?

She pressed her hand to the window and looked over at the front doors to the arena. *Where are you, Rafe? Please be okay. We need you.*

"They're safe enough. For now, I want Mallory Harrigan's thumb drive."

Mallory had a thumb drive? She had no idea what was on it, much less where it was. Zane would have told her if he'd run into one at the rodeo office.

"I... I don't know what you're talking—" Sierra bit her lip. No. Rafe would pretend he knew what the kidnapper was talking about, even if he didn't.

The game was one of perception and expectation. He'd taught her that.

"Don't lie to me, Ms. Bradford. Their lives for the thumb drive. Meet me outside Angel Maker's stall."

"You'll bring Mallory and Chloe?"

"When I receive the thumb drive and verify what's on it, you'll have them back. Agreed?"

Did she have a choice? Zane was too far. Rafe wasn't answering his phone. Maybe she could reach Ransom or Léon.

"I'll be there."

"Come alone, Ms. Bradford. If you call anyone after we hang up, or talk to anyone, they're dead. And I'll know it."

The crack of a gunshot exploded. The window shattered. Sierra fell sideways on the seat. Her phone tumbled to the floorboard.

"Rafe, where are you?"

She glanced around and stared down at her phone. She tapped on the messaging application one last time.

Rafe didn't answer. She was on her own.

Chapter Thirteen

A smattering of gunfire ceased. Rafe had to take the chance while the guy reloaded. He had only seconds and the desk provided little cover. He sprinted to the side wall and flattened his back against a steel cabinet. The shooters kept moving in. If he didn't get a clean shot and take one out to even the odds, the entire situation could get very bad, very fast.

More often than not, this kind of danger gave Rafe a high, but the thought of Sierra and his unborn child in the parking lot gave him cold chills...and a heated fury.

No more iceman.

A grunt and thud sounded from down the hallway. A staccato of gunfire followed.

"Rafe?" a slightly accented voice shouted from the corridor. "One down, one remaining."

A man weaved into the room from the hall, panic on his face. Rafe could see his badge.

He charged at Rafe, weapon drawn and aimed. Damn. Rafe had no choice. He took the shot. The man dropped.

Rafe rushed over to him and knelt beside him. "Who do you work for?"

The guy smiled. "The boss." His head lolled to the side.

"Léon?" Rafe called.

The operative strode over to him, the semi-automatic weapon at his side pointed down. He frowned at the body on the floor, then at Rafe. "Don't you ever answer a call?"

Rafe raised the broken phone. "Sorry. Let me borrow yours. I need to check in with Sierra. She's in the truck."

Léon frowned. "I saw your truck outside."

That cold chill forming over his heart froze over. "Is she okay?"

"She wasn't in the truck, Rafe. It was empty except for a calico cat."

THE STALLS BEHIND the San Antonio Arena were mostly deserted. Sierra walked to one side of a long hallway leading to the bull pens. She stepped carefully and lightly, checking her phone every few seconds, praying that the caller had lied, that Rafe was okay.

Her gun at the ready, she maneuvered behind the empty vendor booths and then ventured across a large dirt-covered training area toward a series of empty stalls.

Empty except for one. Angel Maker.

A loud snort echoed from the bull just as a familiar figure stepped in front of Angel Maker's pen.

She made her way toward him.

John Beckel stared her down. When she was standing maybe ten feet from him, he frowned and crossed his arms. "You brought a gun?"

"I thought it appropriate." She could've kicked herself for not knowing he'd been behind this all the time. Who else could have fixed the books? Who else would want Mallory gone? But she really hadn't thought he had the smarts or the courage to orchestrate this conspiracy.

The bull butted its head against the pen's steel bars. The metal shook. Beckel stepped hastily away from the pen toward her.

Angel Maker slammed into the locked gate again and again and again. Could he break down his cage?

She had no idea.

"A weapon wasn't necessary," John muttered with a scowl. "You've lost weight since I saw you. Another lie. I must say you surprised me. Your husband I could have imagined doing this, but you?" He shrugged, holding a thick envelope in his hand. "I brought your money. As demanded."

He wasn't making any sense. Sierra's brow ruffled. "You contacted me."

A chuckle sounded from behind Sierra. She whirled around.

"You're both wrong. *I* set up this little meeting." Warren Beckel strode toward them, a rifle in his hands. "Lay your weapon on the ground and join my brother, Ms. Bradford. And don't make me shoot you where you stand."

Knowing she had no choice, in slow motion, Sierra knelt down and placed her weapon in the dirt.

"Kick it away."

She followed his instructions, her eyes darting right and left, searching for a way out. If he wanted to shoot, she was an easy target.

He bent and tucked her Glock into the back of his pants.

John started toward his brother, but Warren pointed his rifle at him. "Stay there."

His brother halted. "Warren? What are you doing?"

"Just shut up, John. For once in your life. Your idiotic deal with Diane Manley and her brother cost us everything when you tried—and failed—to hide buying those drugs. You ruined a very sweet deal for me."

"B-but, I'm your brother."

"You're a fool. Always have been. And I'm not bailing you out any longer."

Warren nodded toward Angel Maker. "Walk over to Angel Maker's gate, John."

The man didn't move. He turned ghostly white. His bluster had vanished.

"Do it," Warren said.

Hesitantly, John eased toward the steel structure. He stopped several feet away.

"Unlatch the pen."

The bull eyed John. He tossed his head, snorted and danced around. His hooves spewed dirt into the air.

John backed off. "No. You're cr—"

A shot rang out. John fell to his knees.

"Oh, get up, John. I didn't hit you."

Sierra couldn't stand the taunting any longer. She hurried to the man's side and helped him to his feet. He shook all over and peered at her through sad, resigned eyes. "Warren's going to kill us," he whispered.

Warren pumped the rifle's lever. The metal click echoed like a bullet off the cages. "I won't order you again, John. Unlatch the pen."

With fumbling hands, John lifted the bolt and threw it to the side.

"Get inside. Both of you."

John gripped the top white rod of the gate. "Warren...please. We're family."

"You didn't pull your weight, John. This is how it has to be. Now open the gate and walk inside. I can't explain away a gunshot wound, but I can explain stupidity. I'll play the part well. The distraught brother whose only family, for some reason, entered the den of the beast.

"Do it," Warren ordered.

John swallowed and slowly pulled open the gate. He walked inside.

Sierra hesitated. She'd seen what Angel Maker could do.

Warren's rifle dug into her back. He shoved her forward, then slammed the gate closed behind them.

Angel Maker eyed the intruders, pacing back and forth. Sierra backed against one side of the pen and froze. She couldn't move, could barely breathe. Warren threw the latch down and secured it with a padlock.

Angel Maker snorted. His hoof dug at the dirt. He lowered his head. John panicked. He hitched himself up on the barricade, trying desperately to climb out.

"Don't move," Sierra muttered.

John ignored her. He waved his arms at the bull trying to shoo him away.

It was the wrong move. The bull charged.

Hot breath swept past her. A horn caught John Beckel in the gut. The animal tossed him through the air as if he were a rag doll. John hit the side of the pen, then the ground, his eyes wide and blank.

Sierra blinked. Angel Maker turned on her, snorting anger, his eyes red with fury.

Please don't let it end this way. Please, God, help me save my baby.

MALLORY COULDN'T ESCAPE the thick arm pinning her against a hard chest, or the extra-large hand clamped over her mouth. A football-field length away, the cop who'd threatened to kill her shouted out orders.

"Don't hurt my mommy," Chloe yelled.

The man holding her grunted.

The cop whirled toward them. "That way. Get them!" he shouted.

"Well, damn it, lady."

"You shouldn't cuss—" Chloe said.

Their attacker grabbed her daughter like a football and dragged Mallory a few steps. She cried out in pain and collapsed.

"You're hurt?" His face twisted with regret. Without hesitation, he threw her over his shoulder and ran ten feet behind a pile of construction dirt before letting her go.

"Wh-who are you?" Mallory asked.

"A friend of Sierra's. My name is Zane Westin."

"Is she safe?"

"Worried about you," Zane said, unslinging a mean-looking rifle. He looked down at Chloe with a half smile. "That's a tough little girl you got there, Mrs. Harrigan. She's got a good kick. You a soccer player?"

Chloe nodded. "And T-ball. Did I hurt you?" The question was almost gleeful.

"Absolutely," Zane said, all the while prepping his weapon and laying out extra ammunition.

"I thought you were a bad guy. You got lots of tattoos, and you're really big and you grabbed my mommy hard like my daddy used to when he hurt us."

Mallory flushed red at the revelation, but Zane didn't look at her with judgment, only sympathy.

"Not all big guys with tattoos are bad." He met Mallory's gaze. "Stay behind me, and hide her eyes. We clear?"

"There are so many. Too many."

Zane shrugged and took aim. "Once I cut off the snake's head, the rest of those cowards will fall like dominos." He passed a gun to Mallory.

"It's ready to fire. If anything happens…do what you have to do. Just point and squeeze."

Mallory nodded and pulled Chloe close, hiding the little girl's face in her shoulder.

Zane aimed his weapon. The men racing toward them began shooting. Zane held fast and still. He waited.

Mallory's body tensed. When was he going to shoot? He had plenty of bullets. What if they overran them?

"A few more feet," he muttered. "Just a couple seconds."

He breathed in, exhaled slowly and pulled the trigger. The cop went down with one shot. The men around him skidded to a halt and stared.

The cop didn't move, didn't groan. He'd gone silent.

Zane stood. "I suggest you drop your weapons, gentlemen, or I pick you off one by one."

Glen was the first to surrender. "This ain't worth it." The rest of them followed.

"Mrs. Harrigan, if you could hold this weapon on them, I'll find some cord or rope. We have some bad guys to tie up." Zane paused. "If he moves, just pull the trigger."

Mallory took a deep breath. "I can do that, but you have to get a message to Sierra for me."

Zane nodded. "I'll tell her you're safe."

Mallory shook her head. "No, let her know the thumb drive is in the mouse."

A GUNSHOT ECHOED through the empty arena. Rafe met Léon's furious gaze.

"Sierra!"

Rafe grabbed his weapon, Léon at his side. They raced toward the sound.

When they reached the back of the building, they had two choices: toward the animal pens or offices.

A loud bang decided them. When they hit the open dirt, Rafe skidded to a halt.

Sierra had plastered herself against the side rail inside the pen with Angel Maker. The bull paced opposite her, watching, staring.

"Don't move, honey," Rafe muttered, knowing she couldn't hear him.

Somehow she knew what to do. She stayed still.

A few feet from the pen's gate, Warren Beckel stood watching, a rifle cradled in his elbow.

Rafe would ask himself later how Warren figured into the story, but for now, he had only one mission: to save the mother of his unborn child.

He signaled Léon, and they ducked out of sight.

Léon lifted his sniper rifle, aimed at the pen

and searched through the scope. "One body in the pen. Older guy. He's dead. The gate's padlocked."

"Your weapon won't take down that animal," Rafe said, his adrenaline rushing. The timing had to be perfect, or he'd lose Sierra and the baby. "Even if we create a distraction, she may not be able to climb that fence in time to save herself. She needs me to be her bullfighter."

"I could shoot the padlock. You move in and get her. I'll take out the perp if he makes a move."

"Let's do it."

"It's gonna be a tough shot."

"You have one chance. I trust you Léon."

Rafe circled the dirt area, keeping out of sight. Warren was so focused on the bull and Sierra, he didn't notice.

The closer Rafe moved, the more he could see the bastard's smile. He was enjoying this.

He reached one last barricade twenty feet from Sierra. He'd be out in the open with almost no chance for Warren not to see him. He raised his hand.

Léon fired. Rafe took off running, legs pumping hard.

The padlock exploded.

Rafe barreled into Warren, knocking him off balance.

The bull snorted and charged at Sierra. At the last moment, Rafe wrenched open the metal barrier, grabbed Sierra and pulled her to the side. The bull stormed out and headed straight for Warren. The man staggered up in the center of the open space.

"Run!" Rafe shouted.

The bull lowered his head. The warning came too late.

SEVERAL HOURS LATER night had fallen over San Antonio. Sierra stood inside a small police department conference room with Rafe, looking through a window at chaos. Police, media, politicians.

They were still trying to piece together what had happened. Confusion reigned.

The door opened, and Detective Cade Foster led in Jared King.

"It's a madhouse." Cade walked into the room. "Rafe, do you always cause this much trouble? I got a police captain and patrolman dead. A half dozen thugs coming in from a crime scene several hours from here. A dead veterinarian. Not to mention two deceased

Beckel brothers trampled by a bull. I'm going to be doing paperwork until I retire."

Sierra rushed over to Cade. "Mallory and Chloe?"

"On their way. Hungry and thirsty, but Zane's taking good care of them."

Sierra sagged into her chair. "Thank goodness." She reached for Rafe's hand. "I still don't understand why," she said. "Warren Beckel could have taken control of the rodeo anytime he wanted."

"It wasn't about the rodeo." Rafe flashed a photo of a large steel container.

"Is that a cryostorage tank?" she asked.

Jared King nodded. "This picture from the vet explains a lot. Everything Warren did was about Angel Maker. Or more specifically, the money to be made from his genetic material."

"How?" Sierra asked.

"Angel Maker's *donations* are stored in the tank. Along with scores of other high profile stock animals'. Once he eliminated you and John, Warren planned to kill the bull and claim he did it trying to save you. That would kick the value of the semen he'd collected from Angel Maker ten-, maybe even one-hundred-fold. He already had bidders. Angel Maker was the prize, but adding that to the rest of the stock, he stood to make millions."

"Mallory found out?"

"She didn't know as much as he thought. She found the encrypted file he used to detail transaction information. She didn't know what she had."

"The thumb drive."

A loud knock sounded at the door, and before Cade could open it, Zane strode in carrying a clinging Chloe. Mallory followed on crutches. Sierra broke into a smile and raced over to her friend.

"You're okay. You're alive."

Mallory held her close. "I knew you'd find us. Did you find the thumb drive?"

"Inside Princess Buttercup's toy mouse. Just like you said."

"I wish I'd understood what I had." Mallory frowned. "I was planning to show it to you that night."

Zane lowered Chloe to the floor and sent a very admiring and tender look toward Mallory. "If you hadn't hidden it, no telling what that crazy cop would've done."

Chloe pulled on Sierra's top. "Where's Princess Buttercup?"

"I'll get her," Rafe said, and strode out of the room.

Sierra bent and gave Chloe a hug. "I missed you, Button."

"Those bad men took us away to a yucky place, Sierra."

"I know."

"Zane said you sent him to save me and Mommy." She looked up adoringly at him. "Mommy and I are going to keep him. He belongs to us now."

Mallory flushed even redder, and to Sierra's amusement so did Zane. "I see."

Rafe opened the door and crossed the room. "Is this who you're looking for, young lady?"

Chloe giggled and held out her arms. "You're a pirate."

"A pirate who saved my life." Sierra smiled at Rafe, hoping he saw so much more than she said aloud. "In more ways than one."

Rafe squeezed her hand.

Chloe squinted at them. "You should keep him, Sierra. I think he belongs to you."

THE IMPACT OF the San Antonio Rodeo's secrets would be felt for a long time. Rafe shut the door of their motel room. It was late, but so much more needed to be said.

In the past, he would've already skipped town after a completed job, but Sierra had changed his life. She'd changed everything.

Truthfully it scared the hell out of him—in a good way.

Sierra glanced over at him, and he couldn't stop staring at her. He'd almost lost her. Come so close. He opened his arms and she walked into them.

"I was so scared," she said softly. "Scared for you. For our child."

Rafe licked his lip. "About that…"

A flash of pain crossed her face, and she stiffened.

"Sierra," he said softly. "Don't look away from me."

He cupped her cheeks. "I almost lost you today. Almost lost my last chance at something special, someone special. You're the best thing that's ever happened to me. I won't take that for granted. Not ever again."

"What are you saying?" Her eyes glistened with unshed tears. "I don't want false promises, Rafe. I know this pregnancy is unexpected."

"But not unwanted," he whispered.

She blinked quickly. "Not unwanted."

"I don't know how to convince you how much I want this without telling you something I've never told anyone. Not even Noah." He took a shuddering breath. "About five years ago, I worked with a partner on covert ops. Her name was Gabriella. We were engaged. She was brilliant, like you. Beautiful, like you. A believer in justice, like you."

Sierra shook her head. "I sit behind a computer and track people."

"Give yourself the credit you deserve. You dive into everything headfirst. That Kazakhstan job. You survived Archimedes. You saved Mallory and Chloe. Without you, they wouldn't be here." He grimaced. "Your courage is why Noah and I asked Ransom to bench you. He was afraid for the sister he loves. I was afraid… for you. And I didn't want to lose you. Not like I lost Gabriella."

Sierra wrapped her arms around his waist and squeezed tight. "What happened?"

"Without going into classified details, Gabriella and I trusted the wrong contacts. We were betrayed. The operation caused so many deaths. Including Gabriella's. I ended up in military prison as a traitor."

Shaking her head, she pulled back and met his gaze. "You'd never betray our country. Not ever."

Rafe's throat thickened, and he could barely swallow. "Thank you for that. Until you, only Ransom and Noah truly believed me. They were able to prove reasonable doubt so I was acquitted, but my career was over."

He pulled her closer, wanting to feel her

warmth against him. He looked down into her glittering blue eyes. "My missions were dangerous. I couldn't bear to risk anyone else I cared about. That's why I pushed you away." He cleared his throat. "But even then I couldn't let you go."

He pulled a gold necklace from his pocket and dropped it into her palm.

"My mother's locket," she said. "I thought I'd lost it."

"I found it on the floor of our room two months ago. The chain was broken. I fixed it, but I…couldn't seem to work up the courage to face you. I was afraid I'd never leave you if I saw you again. I couldn't admit, even to myself, that I'd fallen in love with you, Sierra."

Tears rolled down her face. "You l-love me?"

"I don't deserve you, but if you'll forgive me for leaving you, forgive me for all the mistakes I've made and the mistakes I will make, I'll do everything in my power to make you happy, to be a good father. Maybe even earn your love someday."

She set her hands on his shoulders and looked into his eyes. "I love you, Rafe Vargas. I have for a long time. For so many reasons. Because you're a man who would do anything to protect the people in your life, but mostly because of your gentle heart hidden inside the soul of a warrior."

Rafe's arms closed around her. He couldn't stop trembling. "I'm never letting you go again, Sierra. You're my family now. Always and forever."

His lips lowered to hers, and he kissed her with all the passion and love he'd never allowed himself to feel before this moment.

Her breathing grew quick and heavy. His body hardened. He swung her into his arms. "Are you ready to start our life? You and me, together?"

She grinned up at him. "So, which one of us gets to tell Noah?"

Epilogue

Noah and Lyssa's wedding reception was in full swing. Rafe stood out of sight and silently observed their first dance as husband and wife.

He was used to standing on the outside of events like this. Normally he liked to tip his hat and vanish into the night. Celebrations weren't his thing, but that was about to change.

His life was about to transform, and he couldn't be more ready. Except for one small item. His best friend.

He met Sierra's gaze across the crowded reception. She stood with her brother Chase, the only single Bradford left—not that he knew that yet—and her father. Even though Paul Bradford was wheelchair-bound, he knew how to party. He took turns giving his grandkids rides on his chair, a huge smile on his face.

Rafe tugged at the collar on his best man's

tux. How could a simple shirt and tie feel like a choke hold?

The wedding waltz swelled to the final chords. Noah dipped his new bride and followed the move with a passionate kiss.

Applause filled the room, and the band started into another song. A sea of wedding guests invaded the dance floor. Rafe shifted and adjusted his patch.

A small tug pulled at his coat. He glanced down. Joshua Bradford, Mitch's four-year-old adopted son, gazed up at him.

"Are you a pirate?"

Rafe chuckled and shook his head. "Nope, but I can do magic."

He pulled a yo-yo out of his pocket. Within minutes, he'd performed Rock the Baby and Shoot the Moon to an audience of Bradford cousins with openmouthed stares.

The kids whispered to each other, and Joshua, who was obviously the leader stepped forward. "Will you teach us?"

He spent the next half hour working with the kids in the corner before they scampered off for a snack, and yes, avoiding the Bradford family. Yep, he was a coward when it came to Sierra's father and brothers.

Delaying the inevitable.

They hadn't told anyone else about the

baby yet, but Rafe had to wonder if Sierra's sisters-in-law knew. They kept giving him these strange, secret looks.

With his audience vanished, he stood deserted in the corner of the room.

Sierra made her way over to him, smiling in that way that made his belly turn and his body harden. She leaned against him, her warm softness providing him a certainty and comfort he longed for. "You're hiding out," she whispered in his ear, threading her fingers through his.

He turned her to him. "Maybe."

"It'll be okay. I'll protect you." She smiled. "I can handle my family. And Noah."

"You can handle anything."

A small tap poked Rafe. He turned and faced a grinning Chloe. Mallory stood behind her daughter. Zane's arm encircled her, his posture protective and very possessive. Now why didn't that surprise him?

Rafe smiled down at the little girl. "How're you doing, short stuff? Taking good care of your mommy and P.B.?"

"I'm not short." Chloe dug her toe into the wooden floor. "I know you miss Princess Buttercup. I don't want you and Sierra to be lonely when you go home, so I got you a present."

Very slowly and deliberately Chloe handed Rafe a white box. "Be careful."

"This is for us?" Rafe asked with a smile.

"'Cause you saved my Sierra and sent Zane to rescue me and Mommy and took really good care of Princess Buttercup." She cleared her throat. "I mean, P.B."

"You didn't have to give us a present, Chloe."

"Yes, I did. It was my idea." She puffed out her chest. "Open it."

He untied the blue ribbon and pulled off the top. Inside, a small calico kitten blinked up at him.

Rafe reached inside. His throat closed up a bit. The small creature batted her paws at Rafe's fingers. He cleared his throat. "What's her name?"

Chloe gave him a wide grin. "Princess Gingersnap!"

Rafe let out a loud cough, and Chloe erupted into giggles.

"Not really," she said with a smile. "Pirates don't have princess cats. I named her Jelly. 'J' for short. 'Cause they're going to be friends."

"P.B. and J," Rafe said, and swung Chloe into his arms. "She's perfect."

Chloe hugged his neck and whispered in his ear. "Now you and Sierra can be a family, like me and Mommy and Zane."

Rafe set her down. "I'll take good care of Jelly, Chloe. I promise."

The little girl scampered away. Zane gave him a wink and led Mallory away.

Rafe stared down at the kitten in his arms. He met Sierra's gaze, and she finally broke down. Her laughter pealed across the room.

"Go ahead, laugh it up. But we both get to take care of Jelly."

Noah crossed over to them. "Seems like you've developed a soft side, good buddy."

"Can't a guy get a pet without an inquisition?" Rafe asked.

"You don't have to pretend," Noah said. His expression turned solemn. "I trust you like a brother. Always have." He met Rafe's gaze. "Always will."

Though a little concerned where the conversation might be going, Rafe nodded. "Me, too. You had my back when no one else did. I won't forget it."

Noah shook his hand. "You have a chance to make a very good thing official. Don't blow it."

Rafe stared after his best friend, stunned just as Sierra slipped her hand into Rafe's.

"See, it's going to be fine. Besides, they're going to find out sooner or later," she whispered. "About everything."

Rafe rubbed the base of his neck. "I know, but I wanted to do it right. Like you deserve,"

Rafe said, staring into the cobalt eyes of the woman who owned his heart.

"Do you love me?" she asked, with a tilt of her head.

His heart thudded against his chest. "You know I do."

"Then, that's all I need."

She grabbed his hand and led him to the stage. She whispered to one of the band members, and the musicians let loose a musical flourish.

Sierra took the microphone and smiled. "I know this is Noah and Lyssa's big day. I'm so happy for them, but I have a little something to say, and I wanted to share it with the people I love most in the world, who are all in this room."

Rafe could feel his face flushing. Paul Bradford rolled his chair right up to the bandstand. Noah and Lyssa, Mitch and Emily and Chase stood behind him.

Sierra knelt in front of Rafe and pulled a box out of her pocket. "Rafe Vargas. I love you. I want to spend the rest of my life with you, as my partner, my best friend, the father of my children, and the other half of my heart. Will you marry me?"

Rafe froze. A tear burned behind his eye. He glanced over at a grinning sea of faces, including Noah. His friend didn't even jump up on the stage to slug him. He simply smiled like he'd known all along.

What an irritating quality for a brother-in-law.

"Yes. Yes. Yes," the room chanted.

Rafe knew in that moment what he had to do. He faced Sierra and knelt down. He pulled a velvet box out of his pocket and flipped it open. A sapphire and diamond engagement ring the color of her eyes gleamed in the black velvet.

"You stole my line," he whispered to her, lifting her hand and slipping on the ring. "I wanted to surprise you."

A deafening wave of applause clamored through the room. Rafe didn't hear a sound. He cupped Sierra's face and lowered his lips slowly, tenderly to hers, wrapped her in his arms and kissed her with all the world watching.

"We'll tell them about the baby later," she whispered against his mouth.

"Much later," he said softly, and kissed her again.

No more secrets. No more lies.

Just love.

* * * * *

LARGER-PRINT BOOKS!

♦HARLEQUIN *Presents®*

GET 2 FREE LARGER-PRINT NOVELS PLUS 2 FREE GIFTS!

YES! Please send me 2 FREE LARGER-PRINT Harlequin Presents® novels and my 2 FREE gifts (gifts are worth about $10). After receiving them, if I don't wish to receive any more books, I can return the shipping statement marked "cancel." If I don't cancel, I will receive 6 brand-new novels every month and be billed just $5.30 per book in the U.S. or $5.74 per book in Canada. That's a saving of at least 12% off the cover price! It's quite a bargain! Shipping and handling is just 50¢ per book in the U.S. and 75¢ per book in Canada.* I understand that accepting the 2 free books and gifts places me under no obligation to buy anything. I can always return a shipment and cancel at any time. Even if I never buy another book, the two free books and gifts are mine to keep forever.

176/376 HDN GHVY

Name	(PLEASE PRINT)	
Address		Apt. #
City	State/Prov.	Zip/Postal Code

Signature (if under 18, a parent or guardian must sign)

Mail to the **Reader Service**:
IN U.S.A.: P.O. Box 1867, Buffalo, NY 14240-1867
IN CANADA: P.O. Box 609, Fort Erie, Ontario L2A 5X3

**Are you a subscriber to Harlequin Presents® books
and want to receive the larger-print edition?
Call 1-800-873-8635 today or visit us at www.ReaderService.com.**

* Terms and prices subject to change without notice. Prices do not include applicable taxes. Sales tax applicable in N.Y. Canadian residents will be charged applicable taxes. Offer not valid in Quebec. This offer is limited to one order per household. Not valid for current subscribers to Harlequin Presents Larger-Print books. All orders subject to credit approval. Credit or debit balances in a customer's account(s) may be offset by any other outstanding balance owed by or to the customer. Please allow 4 to 6 weeks for delivery. Offer available while quantities last.

Your Privacy—The Reader Service is committed to protecting your privacy. Our Privacy Policy is available online at www.ReaderService.com or upon request from the Reader Service.

We make a portion of our mailing list available to reputable third parties that offer products we believe may interest you. If you prefer that we not exchange your name with third parties, or if you wish to clarify or modify your communication preferences, please visit us at www.ReaderService.com/consumerchoice or write to us at Reader Service Preference Service, P.O. Box 9062, Buffalo, NY 14240-9062. Include your complete name and address.

HPLP15

LARGER-PRINT BOOKS!

GET 2 FREE LARGER-PRINT NOVELS PLUS
2 FREE GIFTS!

◆HARLEQUIN®

Romance

From the Heart, For the Heart

YES! Please send me 2 FREE LARGER-PRINT Harlequin® Romance novels and my 2 FREE gifts (gifts are worth about $10). After receiving them, if I don't wish to receive any more books, I can return the shipping statement marked "cancel." If I don't cancel, I will receive 4 brand-new novels every month and be billed just $5.09 per book in the U.S. or $5.49 per book in Canada. That's a savings of at least 15% off the cover price! It's quite a bargain! Shipping and handling is just 50¢ per book in the U.S. and 75¢ per book in Canada.* I understand that accepting the 2 free books and gifts places me under no obligation to buy anything. I can always return a shipment and cancel at any time. Even if I never buy another book, the two free books and gifts are mine to keep forever.

119/319 HDN GHWC

Name	(PLEASE PRINT)	
Address		Apt. #
City	State/Prov.	Zip/Postal Code

Signature (if under 18, a parent or guardian must sign)

Mail to the Reader Service:
IN U.S.A.: P.O. Box 1867, Buffalo, NY 14240-1867
IN CANADA: P.O. Box 609, Fort Erie, Ontario L2A 5X3

Want to try two free books from another line?
Call 1-800-873-8635 or visit www.ReaderService.com.

* Terms and prices subject to change without notice. Prices do not include applicable taxes. Sales tax applicable in N.Y. Canadian residents will be charged applicable taxes. Offer not valid in Quebec. This offer is limited to one order per household. Not valid for current subscribers to Harlequin Romance Larger-Print books. All orders subject to credit approval. Credit or debit balances in a customer's account(s) may be offset by any other outstanding balance owed by or to the customer. Please allow 4 to 6 weeks for delivery. Offer available while quantities last.

Your Privacy—The Reader Service is committed to protecting your privacy. Our Privacy Policy is available online at www.ReaderService.com or upon request from the Reader Service.

We make a portion of our mailing list available to reputable third parties that offer products we believe may interest you. If you prefer that we not exchange your name with third parties, or if you wish to clarify or modify your communication preferences, please visit us at www.ReaderService.com/consumerchoice or write to us at Reader Service Preference Service, P.O. Box 9062, Buffalo, NY 14240-9062. Include your complete name and address.

HRLP15

LARGER-PRINT BOOKS!
GET 2 FREE LARGER-PRINT NOVELS PLUS
2 FREE GIFTS!

HARLEQUIN

super romance

More Story...More Romance

HSRLP15

Name	(PLEASE PRINT)	

Address		Apt. #

City	State/Prov.	Zip/Postal Code

Signature (if under 18, a parent or guardian must sign)

Mail to the **Reader Service**:

IN U.S.A.: P.O. Box 1867, Buffalo, NY 14240-1867
IN CANADA: P.O. Box 609, Fort Erie, Ontario L2A 5X3